ABBY'S

a novel

JOURNEY

Also by Steena Holmes

ABBY'S

a novel

JOURNEY

STEENA HOLMES

LAKE UNION
PUBLISHING

Published by Lake Union Publishing, Seattle

www.apub.com

Amazon, the Amazon logo, and Lake Union Publishing are trademarks of Amazon.com, Inc., or its affiliates.

ISBN-13: 9781503940321
ISBN-10: 1503940322

Cover design by Shasti O'Leary Soudant

Printed in the United States of America

To all my fellow travelholics:
May your souls be filled with wanderlust and a need to
explore the world. And remember, living with passion
and pursuing your dreams is a life well lived.

PROLOGUE

CLAIRE

Dear Josh,

I've written this letter a thousand times (okay, that might be exaggerating just a little, but I have written it a few times now). At first, it was a list of parenting tips, because that's what I do, I write lists. And then you would read it and memorize it, because that's what you do to humor me.

But then I realized that I don't want the last letter I write to you to be solely a display of my inner control freak. But Josh, the list is a good one. It really is. So how about this—I'll add it to the end of this letter on a separate sheet, so you can post it on the fridge or leave it on your desk, somewhere you can reference it when things get too hard.

You won't be alone in raising Abby. I don't imagine Millie leaving your side for the first little bit. No doubt she'll be one of those grandmas (or maybe she prefers nana?) who spoil babies. Which is probably okay. A little bit of spoiling can't hurt, right? Call Abigail anytime you're worried about the sniffles or if she gets a fever. And let Derek drag you out of the house so you can breathe.

You can do this. I know you can, even without my lists. You'll be amazing at raising our little girl. She's lucky to have you, Josh. She really is. No one will love her like you will, no one will protect her like you will, and no one will teach her what it is to love others the way you will.

Keep her safe. Make sure she grows up healthy and happy. Share your stories with her, your dreams, take her on trips, and show her the world. Please? For me? (Yes, I'm seriously asking you to do this for me—share my love for travel with our daughter. That would mean everything to me.) Take her on her own personal Jack's Adventures tour, like we've talked about. Show her where we came up with story ideas—and maybe make up a few new ones?

I love you, Joshua Turner.

I love you, and I've always chosen you, every moment of my life since you swept me off my feet with your boyish charm and your passion for exploring the world around us. I will always remember when you showed me your own list of what you wanted in life. And despite how . . . boyish it was (I still can't believe you put keggers and swamp-buggy racing on there), I knew right then and there we were soul mates.

Now, about that list I mentioned earlier . . .

Here's my last official list for you. Maybe also think about reading those parenting magazines I bought two-year subscriptions for (and when it comes time to renew, renew—it's what I would do).

Do laundry at least once a week (probably more with a baby in the house).

Pack nutritious lunches.

It's okay to let our child dress herself. Inside out, backward—it's all good. Maybe ask Abigail for help when buying clothes, though.

Hats, mitts, and scarfs are a necessity. Not optional. Keep Abby healthy. The fewer colds, the better. Same with rain boots, winter boots, etc.

Coffee is okay as a teenager (I drank it before I was sixteen, and I survived), but Millie will probably recommend tea first.

Don't forget multivitamins. For both you and our girl.

Say I love you *every day!*

Deal with situations after the anger has passed.

Find something to laugh about each day.

Ask Millie to teach you how to braid her hair and put it in ponytails.

Bath time is essential every night. Followed by story time.

Once puberty hits, talk to Abigail. Panty liners, tampons, pads—you know the drill.

On that note, ask Abigail to take her bra shopping too.

Tea parties are important.

Don't be a helicopter parent (see the shelves of parenting books in my office—there's a lot in there for you to peruse).

Don't attempt to be perfect all the time. If you miss a bath or two—oh, well. She'll survive.

Change the bedsheets at least once a month (every week is preferable).

Never stop hugging her, even if, when she's a teen, she shies away. She's always going to need hugs from you.

Don't forget to take care of yourself too—when you need a break, call in reinforcements (a.k.a. Derek).

Don't share only your chocolate obsession with our daughter. Make sure she falls in love with coconut cream cake too!

Make time for fun.

Teach her responsibility, but don't put too much pressure on her too soon either.

Don't go to bed angry with her. Teach her while she's young, and this'll come naturally in her future relationships.

Listen with an open mind and heart when she talks about her first crush. Don't make her afraid to talk to you about boys.

Read to her every night. And when she's old enough, let her read to you as well.

Most importantly, don't ever forget that I love you, that having a child with you was my heart's true wish, and that I trust you completely.

See . . . that wasn't too bad, was it?

ONE

CLAIRE

To be read on Mother's Day when you are eighteen.

Dear Abby,

It's a mother's sworn duty to share her wisdom with her child, and it's the child's responsibility to heed her mother's guidance and live her life by its light.

So with that in mind, I have some words of advice for you. Three words, to be exact.

Dream. Cherish. Love.

Don't ever stop dreaming, my love.

Don't be afraid to dream great things—things you think are beyond your grasp.

Trust me. I know what I'm talking about. If I'd given up on my dream for a baby, you wouldn't be here. And honestly, I can't imagine that.

Push yourself to dream bigger, with more breadth and passion than at first you dare to hope.

Cherish those little moments that linger in your mind and, when you least expect it, magically unfurl into . . . something more. It was in moments like those that I fell in love with your father, that I knew I wanted to travel the world and hear people's stories, that I decided to pursue drawing as a career. Don't skip over or hurry past those moments. Your life grows from them.

Through loving others, be an inspiration to everyone around you, Abby.

I know you're amazing and so full of light and laughter. Let all of this, all of who you are, shine through your smile and your actions.

Forever and always,

Mom, who loves you to the moon and back, who never stopped dreaming of you, who loved you even before she knew about you . . . and who will always love you

TWO

JOSH

After twenty years, living without Claire should have gotten easier, but it never had.

And Christmastime made the loneliness . . . so much worse.

It wasn't that he was a *bah humbug* kind of a guy, but—well, he was now.

That's what happened when eighteen times out of twenty, his daughter's sniffles turned into pneumonia; when nineteen out of twenty Christmas Eves were spent in the children's ward, watching his daughter struggle to breathe; and when twenty out of twenty Christmas mornings, he forced himself to smile, to go through the motions of believing there was any magic at all in the holidays.

It was hard to see the merry when all you felt was sorry—for yourself, for your child, for what could have been.

If it weren't for his daughter, he'd seclude himself at the cabin until the holiday was over. He'd be a happy man if he never again strung a set of Christmas lights around the house, decorated a tree, or watched a cheesy Christmas movie.

"'Suck it up, buttercup.' That's what you'd say if you were here, wouldn't you, Claire?"

He still spoke to his dead wife, even after all these years. Some might call him pathetic. Or a sad case. He didn't care. If it weren't for his daughter, he had no doubt he'd have died of a broken heart years ago.

But, he had to be strong for Abby, for the sake of her health. In that first year alone, she had survived bacterial pneumonia, a collapsed lung, and multiple infections. Many times Dr. Blackwood had told him Abby was in a fragile state, that their goal was to make her comfortable, and yet miracle followed miracle, and his little girl continued to fight.

If she could do it, so could he. That thought kept him going—it was how he survived those early years, without Claire at his side.

Without her, everything changed.

For the first ten years of Abby's life, he hadn't been able to write. He'd tried so many times, revisiting all the places that used to spark his creativity—doodling in his notebook at the patio table, gazing across the bay from his favorite rocky perch at the nature reserve, and even sitting at Claire's desk in her office, where she used to work, gazing out the window that overlooked their backyard. But neither words nor stories would come. His publisher had looked into hiring a new illustrator for the books, but none of the portfolios she sent over inspired him. No one else's art could replace Claire's drawings. No matter how hard he'd tried, the sentences wouldn't flow. Every word was a struggle and each description fell flat, until he'd had to accept reality. There would be no more Jack's Adventures children's books without Claire.

It had taken him a long time to discover who he was without her. She wasn't just his life mate but his business partner, his best friend, his other half in everything.

So while Abby lived in a little incubator for months, he mourned her loss.

While Abby lay in her hospital bed, hooked up to monitors and equipment that helped her lungs breathe and her heart beat, he worked through what it meant to be a man without his soul mate.

And once Abby was finally able to come home, to sleep for the first time in her own bed, surrounded by the stuffed animals she called friends, he began learning how to be a single parent to this little girl with an unquenchable will to live.

As he well knew, single parenting was not for the faint of heart. Especially when raising a strong-willed, independent daughter who is certain she knows what she wants in life and wants it right now. Despite how hard life had been when she was a child, he would give anything to turn back the clock, if it meant he would not have to deal with *this*.

"Can we at least talk about it?" Abby slouched against the wall, her arms tight across her chest.

Josh glanced down at his watch. "We've been talking about it for the last hour. I'm pretty firm in my decision, Abby."

Keep calm. Keep calm. Do not lose your shit. Keep calm. He repeated that to himself, while his daughter stood there, staring straight into his eyes. He knew what she was doing. This Jedi-mind trick of hers wasn't new. She thought if she waited him out, he'd change his mind.

But not this time.

She was ready to move out and live with her friend Samantha. Away from him and his rules and his—what was the word she used? *Protectiveness.*

She actually accused him of being too protective.

"You're not listening to me, Dad."

Josh's leg bounced restlessly. "I'm listening Abby. I've been listening. I can listen and still disagree. In fact, I could say the same about you, that you're the one not listening to a word I've said."

Abby pushed herself from the wall and walked over to the counter. She yanked the cupboard open and slammed a mug down on the counter so hard Josh thought the cup would break.

"I'm not a little kid anymore," she huffed.

He watched as she began to wheeze, and he glanced repeatedly at the inhaler on the counter. He waited for her to pick it up and use it. Eventually she did.

Abby lived with BPD—bronchopulmonary dysplasia—which meant her lungs were weak due to her premature birth and she often had difficulty breathing. It also meant that she was particularly susceptible to getting colds. More often than not, a runny nose or cough would develop into full-blown pneumonia, requiring a trip to the hospital.

"If you're not a kid, then stop acting like one." He hated it when she was so stubborn. He needed to go for a run, to burn off some of his frustration.

Abby whirled around with a look of incredulity on her face, and for a second, Josh wanted to smile. She looked so much like her mother right then.

Josh rose to refill his coffee.

"Okay. Maybe we're both a little too emotional right now about this. Why don't we take a breather—say, an hour? I'll go for a run, and you go do whatever you need to do, preferably bake more of those cookies you made earlier this week." He gave her a smile. "Then we'll meet back here and talk some more."

During Abby's childhood and into her teen years, this was a tactic he'd learned was useful whenever things got heated between them. It was actually Millie who had given him the idea when she'd tried it one day after walking in on the two of them arguing over a sweater Abby wanted. He thought the price was ridiculous and said as much, and Abby had ended up in tears. Millie saved the day by calling a time-out. Then she coaxed them into resuming the discussion a bit later, once they were both calmer, and they'd struck a deal. Abby got her sweater, but she bought it with her own money.

"And you'll listen?" Abby asked, a gleam of hope in her eyes.

"Sell me on why your moving out is a good idea. I'll listen." He didn't like conflict between them, didn't like when they couldn't see eye to eye. And lately, it was happening all too frequently.

He got it. She wasn't a child anymore. She was twenty and wanted to experience life, not stay cooped up at home with her father always watching over her. Except, he wasn't sure if she was ready.

He wasn't sure if *he* was ready. He cringed inwardly.

He gave her a small kiss on the forehead and ran up the stairs to change into running clothes. A few miles of feet hitting the ground should clear his head.

❖ ❖ ❖

An hour and a shower later, Josh walked into the kitchen to the smell of chocolate haystack cookies. He spied a few on a plate and popped one into his mouth. He loved when his daughter baked, especially when she made his favorite snacks.

He'd expected to see her down here, waiting for him, but she was nowhere to be found. He'd already looked in her room and in Claire's office, she wasn't in the living room, and she wouldn't be outside.

She wouldn't be outside . . . And yet he found himself walking toward the window and looking into their backyard, where he discovered his daughter standing in the middle of a pile of snow, face tilted up, with the most peaceful smile on her face he'd seen in a while.

He pounded on the glass and gestured her back into the house. What was she thinking? Thank God she had her jacket on along with her scarf, mitts, and hat, but still . . .

"I didn't know you were back," Abby said a little sheepishly as she hung up her jacket in the mudroom where he waited.

"So this is normal then? You sneaking outside in the middle of winter when you know you shouldn't?" He could feel his blood pressure rising.

"I just wanted some fresh air, and I wasn't out long. Feel." She came toward him and offered her hands. "They're not even cold."

His eyebrows rose. He ignored the hands that shouldn't be cold because they had been covered with warm wool, and instead he placed his hands on her face, covering the bright red cheeks that livened her face. He frowned.

"Why don't you go stand in front of the fireplace while I put the kettle on?" That he managed to keep his voice even and calm more than amazed him.

"It's the perfect day to build a snowman, don't you think? Or go to the market in town? I'm sure there would be hot chocolate there to warm us up, and . . ." Her voice trailed off when she saw the response on his face.

"Fine. I'll go stand in front of the fire like a good little girl and wait for you to make us tea." She turned and clomped toward the front room, her footsteps resounding against the floor.

He watched her walk away. If Claire were here, she would have joined Abby outside and made all the snowmen and snow angels their daughter desired. She'd also be at the market every weekend, helping run things, passing out those pocket-sized hand warmers, and wishing everyone a merry Christmas, while their daughter flitted about, talking up a storm to anyone and everyone she encountered.

He could see it all clearly, as though it were true.

Unless their daughter was sick. Then Claire would be doing exactly what he was doing now.

Being overly cautious.

This was how he made it as a single dad—thinking about what Claire would do if she hadn't died minutes after giving birth to their daughter.

During the time it took for the kettle to boil and the tea to steep, he calmed down, somewhat. He didn't enjoy arguing with his daughter and usually went out of his way not to. But today it felt like she was pushing all the right buttons.

He carried the tray with their tea and a few haystacks into the living room and found Abby wrapped up in a blanket in the oversized chair, her legs curled up beneath her and her cheeks no longer bright red.

"Thank you for the haystacks." He passed a mug of tea to her before making himself comfortable on the couch.

"I was hoping they would sweeten you up a bit," Abby said.

He laughed. "Was that before or after you decided to go sit outside in the cold?"

"It's not that cold. You went out for a run with only a pullover and sweats on."

"I'm not the one who is sick," he said pointedly.

"I'm not sick."

He didn't bother to argue with her. They were waiting on her latest clinical assessment and X-rays for her BPD, but until then, he'd do everything he could to ensure she didn't get sick again.

It never took much.

His mind flashed back to the times he'd given in, because he'd wanted Abby to have a normal childhood, and his decisions had ended up backfiring terribly.

Like the time he took her to the local outdoor skating rink when she was seven so he could teach her how to skate, and she came home with a runny nose, which became a chest cold that by the middle of the night left her almost unable to breathe.

Or the time when she was fifteen and had begged to go white-water rafting during a summer camping trip, only to wake up the following morning with the sniffles, which turned into pneumonia so quickly he barely got her home in time for treatment. Summer colds were the worst—and she'd almost died. He still had nightmares over that one.

But he would also never forget the look of sheer joy on her face when he'd built her a snow family in the front yard when she was five.

She'd been lying on the couch watching her favorite Disney movie when he came in and drew back the curtains, revealing the winter scene he'd made to surprise her. She couldn't go out to build her own snowmen, but he could do it for her.

It was a sad truth, but he had more memories of Abby being sick than well.

"Can we talk now?" Abby asked, her hands wrapped tight around her tea mug. "I've thought about what you said, and I have some ideas."

"I'm listening."

"The issue is that I want to go to school in Toronto, and you're concerned that I'm not ready, right?" Abby began.

Josh shrugged in reply. She'd applied and been accepted to several colleges behind his back.

"If the concern is that I'll get sick again and you won't be there to take care of me, then one of the selling points to me moving out is that I'll be closer to Dr. JJ."

"Aunt Abigail, who is also a doctor, is literally a ten-minute drive from us. I doubt you'll live that close to Dr. JJ or to the hospital."

Abby's brow furrowed. "True, but I won't be alone. I'll be with Sam."

Sam was Abby's best friend and old enough to be her big sister. Josh had met Sam, or Sami as she'd been called when she was younger, at a book signing in Toronto with Claire. She and Claire had bonded, and Josh had stayed in touch with Sam even after Claire died. She'd been a constant companion to Abby growing up, and he'd been so thankful for that throughout the years.

"Sam has never lived on her own either. She has her own share of health concerns."

Sam was legally blind. If she looked closely and stared long enough, she could discern shapes and muted colors, but even then, things weren't all that clear for her. She had a guide dog to help and a boyfriend, who rarely left her side. But that wasn't enough for Josh to be okay with this.

"Right." Abby nodded and took a deep breath. "But her mother found us a small apartment that is literally around the corner from her, which makes her even closer than Aunt Abigail."

"Well. That is good." Josh would give her that one.

"Sam really wants to move out, Dad. She wants some independence before she and Dean get engaged. She needs it, and really, what better companion could I have than Sam? You know her mom won't let her move out on her own. She's just as protective as you are. And if it's a matter of safety, there's her dog."

"Sam's dog is meant for Sam. Not for you. But, I do hear what you're saying."

A hint of a smile appeared on his daughter's face. "So does that mean . . . ?"

He shook his head. He hated to disappoint her, but the bottom line was that until he knew with certainty that she was okay from a medical standpoint, he wasn't going to agree to her moving out. She'd been homeschooled and done well. Why couldn't she get her bachelor's degree the same way? Or attend the college where he taught?

Abby fidgeted with the blanket on her lap. "Come on, Dad." She raised her gaze. "Don't you think it's time to stop—"

"Being so protective?" He knew where she was going with this. He would never apologize, if that was what she was looking for.

"No," she said, shaking her head, "being scared. I'm not Mom, and I don't have cancer."

"No, you don't have cancer." He let the words sit there between them, and then he looked over at a photo of Claire that sat on the bookshelf behind Abby. "But I can't count how many times I almost lost you too." He shook his head, unwilling to let the memories cocoon him.

"You're not losing me now, though. I'm just . . . growing up."

"I want my little girl back. You remember her, right? The one who used to snuggle with me on the couch while watching movies—and who never argued with her wise father." He tried for humor, but his voice gave him away. Josh swallowed hard past the lump in his throat. He knew he couldn't get too emotional or she'd win—he'd let her move in with Sam before he knew for sure that she was okay.

"You're the best dad a girl could ever have. You know that, right?" Abby came over to the couch and sat beside him. "I just"—she rested her head on his shoulder—"I just want to live life, you know? I'm twenty, and I feel like I've barely lived at all."

To Josh, it felt like a punch to the gut, the way Abby said it was so painfully reminiscent of Claire. "I just want to make sure you live long enough to experience life, that's all." He forced himself to smile. "Give your old man a break, okay? I'm not saying no, just that we need to wait till we hear from Dr. JJ. Can you give me that, at least? Let's see what the tests say."

When she looked up at him, there was a soft smile on her face.

"Thank you," she said quietly.

He leaned over and placed a kiss on her forehead.

They stayed like that for a few minutes before she sat up. "That reminds me, my sleep app shows I'm in the 90 percent range for my target. Which means I'm getting enough rest." Her shoulders straightened with the news.

"That's great."

"I know, right? I'm determined to win our little bet. Who knew sleep would be the key to staying healthy?"

He swiveled to look at her. "Not just the sleep. How about taking your vitamins regularly and the tea David brings around? I'm sure that's helping too."

"It's the sleep, Dad. I know it. I've been reading up on a bunch of sleep studies that have been done. Did you know that reading on your devices disrupts your sleep cycle? It has to do with the blue light. Which is why you shouldn't be staying up so late reading on your tablet." She gave him a playful nudge with her elbow.

"Don't drag me into this, kiddo."

"I'm just saying shutting down your screen at a decent hour and getting a good eight to ten hours wouldn't hurt."

"I get enough sleep, thank you very much. You just worry about yourself. Glad the sleep app is keeping track, though. You'll have to share that with your aunt when you see her next."

"Do we have any plans for tonight?"

"No. Why?"

"It's the last night of the market, and I haven't seen it at night this year. Could we go? Just for a quick walk around the park?"

"Not until we hear back regarding your test results. Dr. JJ warned it could take a few days." He shook his head.

Her shoulders slumped forward, and that magical sparkle disappeared.

"I feel fine, Dad. The results will come back telling you exactly that, and you'll have kept me locked in this house for nothing. Honestly, what are you going to do when I move out?"

"Who says you are?" He gave her what he hoped was a don't-mess-with-me look.

She rolled her eyes.

"Come on, let's finish our tea and watch a movie. How about *The Avengers*?"

"Again? I vote not. How about *The Princess Bride* or *13 Going on 30*?" This time it was his turn to roll his eyes.

"I'm pretty sure there's a *Die Hard* movie on. Let's watch that instead." He went to grab the remote, but she beat him to it.

"I'm serious. You realize that, right?" Abby situated herself on the couch, tucking the blanket around her as she did so.

"I'm pretty sure we're talked out about this, aren't we? Didn't we just agree to wait until we hear back from Dr. JJ?"

"It's been almost a year since I was last sick," she reminded him.

"Which is why you had that pulmonary function test and X-ray and why we're waiting to hear back from her before a decision is made. Come on, Claire—can we just drop it now? Please?"

Until this year, she'd never gone a full twelve months without getting sick. Very sick. She made it eleven months once, a few years ago, before she got hit with a cold that quickly developed into another case of pneumonia. He wasn't expecting a good report from Abby's doctor, JJ Blackwood, this time either.

"Abby," his daughter said softly.

"Sorry?" He was lost.

"My name is Abby," she repeated. "You called me Claire. You do that a lot, Dad."

"Oh, honey, I'm sorry." Did he do it a lot? He had no clue. He wasn't surprised, though. Every day, she reminded him more and more of his wife.

"It's all right." She shrugged before jumping to her feet. "How about some popcorn before the movie starts?" She rushed into the kitchen as her eyes began to tear up. The net of guilt around his heart tightened, squeezing so hard it left permanent marks.

He leaned his head back against the couch and stared up at the ceiling.

"Sorry, love," he whispered. "I'm trying. I really am. It's times like this she needs her mom and I'm a poor substitute."

THREE

CLAIRE

To be read after your first fight with our daughter.

> *Before you do or say anything else, take a deep breath.*
> *Whatever happened, whatever was said, whatever was*
> *done, don't be angry.*
> *Go apologize.*
> *Give her a hug.*
> *Tell her you love her.*
> *Listen to her and let her talk.*
> *Give her the space to be honest with you.*
> *Be honest back . . . but not in a hurtful way.*
> *Don't tear each other apart with words. It's not worth it.*
> *Write her a note if she won't listen to you. Tell her you*
> *love her and want to talk.*
> *You'll fix this. Whatever this is.*
>
> *I never had a good relationship with my father, and*
> *I don't want that for our daughter. Always let her know*
> *that she can come to you with anything and everything,*
> *that you won't judge her or berate her, that you'll love her*
> *and support her, and that you will always be there for her.*

I know, I know—you want to remind me that not everyone has a father like mine, and you're right. Your dad was amazing and such a good influence in your life, which means I don't need to remind you how to be a dad.

I love you.

Claire

FOUR

ABBY

Abby's Journey: A Personal Blog

Another Winter Day

Ever since I was a little girl, I've dreamed of the perfect winter day. I'd spend the day catching snowflakes on my tongue, making snow angels, skating around the pond in our backyard, then drinking hot cocoa by the fireplace after building the biggest snow-man in the world. But, I've always tended to get sick easily—especially when it's cold out. I'm the kid that is wrapped up from head to toe like the abominable snowgirl, where all you can see are my eyes peeking through layers of wool. But even though I'm no lon-ger a kid, I still dream of this perfect day. If I ever have children, they'll be out in the snow, building forts, having snowball fights, making snow angels, drinking hot cocoa,

*and freezing their little ears off—but loving
every minute of it. I'll just have to make sure
I marry a man who can be outside with them
since I doubt my lungs will ever behave, no
matter how old I get.*

*Since I can't be out there in the snow, please
tell me you are . . . pretty please!*

*PS. I think today is the day to try some new
hot chocolate recipes I found online. Stay
tuned.*

Abby never knew her mother. On the day she'd been born, her mother had died, and for her entire twenty years of life, Abby lived with the guilt that it was her fault—even if no one had actually said that. No one needed to. She saw it in all the people who had known her mother, the way their gazes would slide off to the side, their plastered-on smiles, and their forced cheerfulness whenever she mentioned her mom's name.

Her mother, an illustrator and children's book author with many young fans, gave up her life so that Abby could live. After years of trying to get pregnant, she was twelve weeks into her pregnancy when she began experiencing debilitating headaches that turned out to be symptoms of brain cancer. Rather than risk any danger to her baby, Claire had opted not to have surgery or other treatments for the cancer, deciding instead to wait until after Abby was born.

In the end, it hadn't even mattered. Her mother's body had had enough, and just after giving birth, she died from a pulmonary embolism that caused cardiac arrest.

After practically growing up in a hospital due to her weak lungs, Abby had come to realize her mother's body just couldn't handle being pregnant, and that her own chronic illness was penance for being the reason her mom was dead.

Abby's chest tightened at the thought, and she reached automatically for the inhaler she kept in her pocket.

This room had been her mom's sanctuary. She sketched, she wrote, she daydreamed all in this room. The bookshelves lining one wall were full of her favorite novels, framed artwork from those she admired, her journals, and the treasures she'd collected while traveling. The wall opposite her desk was full of postcards from readers all over the world who had fallen in love with the stories her parents had created about a little boy named Jack.

She loved this room, loved to come in here and read or watch one of the videos her mom had recorded for her all those years ago. She loved to daydream in here, to imagine what life could have been like if her mother had lived.

She used to play pretend—that her mom sat at her desk, drawing, while she worked on her homework, or that they'd have heart-to-heart talks about boys and friends and afterward eat a tub of ice cream together in commiseration.

In reality, she sat in the room alone. Always alone. Her dad never came in here. If he needed her, he'd stand at the edge, just outside of the room at the door, not setting even a foot inside. He never gave a reason, and she eventually stopped asking.

Her mother was the love of her father's life, and even though it had been twenty years since her death, he still mourned for her.

Abby hoped to one day find that kind of love too. But, she never would if she remained locked up inside this house, that's for sure.

Her cell phone buzzed, and she smiled at the name on the display.

"Come save me, please," she begged Sam, who was her best friend, aunt, and older sister all rolled into one.

"Where are you?" Sam laughed.

"At home, of course."

Sam laughed even harder. "Your dad still won't let you out of the house, huh? Have your results come back yet?"

"No. But I feel fine." If anyone would understand, it was Sam.

Sam was nine years older than Abby and had beat cancer as a child. Sam had met Claire just months before Abby's birth. It was at one of their readings at a bookstore, and Claire had drawn a picture of Sam as she sat among the other kids listening to Josh's enthusiastic storytelling of a tale from their latest Jack's Adventures book.

"You may feel fine, Abs, but it could sneak up on you. You know that. It's winter. Your lungs hate winter. Have you even once been able to walk outside and breathe cold air without feeling like your lungs were empty?"

"No," Abby grudgingly admitted.

"Then stop complaining and accept what you've always known—you have a chronic lung disease. It could be worse, you know," Sam reminded her.

"I know." Abby thought about the kids she grew up with in the hospital. Some of them lived on ventilators because their lungs were so weak. Some didn't survive their latest round of pneumonia. Sam was right. She needed to stop complaining.

"Fine," Abby said. "Then come over, and let's book a flight to a tropical island where there's never any snow."

Sam snorted over the phone.

"I'm serious." Abby let out a long sigh. "I'm sitting in my mom's office and looking at her wall of postcards. In all her letters and videos to me, she keeps saying she hopes I will travel, that I'll fall in love with faraway places."

"Maybe you'll be able to, one day," Sam said.

Abby stood in front of her mother's giant corkboard, where she had arrayed postcards from various places she'd visited herself or places friends had sent a postcard from. All Abby's favorite ones were from Europe.

She lightly brushed one particular postcard with her fingers. This was the one she loved best. It was an image of the *Christkindlmarkt* in Nuremberg, Germany, and the picture had heart-shaped gingerbread cookies in a frame around it. Every time she saw this postcard, it was like she could smell the gingerbread and hear the jingling bells of a horse-drawn carriage.

"I want to go to Germany," she blurted.

"What? Why there? It's cold."

"I know, but not as cold as here. I checked." She unpinned the postcard and sat back down in her chair. "The German Christmas markets are supposed to be amazing and not to be missed, and they continue for a few weeks past Christmas. Can you imagine how awesome it would be? I could finally actually write about traveling on my blog instead of just dreaming about it. And the photos—think of what I could post on Instagram!" The excitement rose inside of her as she thought about it. She'd be freezing; she'd have to wear mitts, a scarf, and a hat; but she'd be alive and experiencing life like never before.

"Oh, Abby."

"I know, I know." She was dreaming too big. She heard it in Sam's voice.

"Just because we're limited doesn't mean life sucks. I know you think so . . . but give it some time. You'll have a different perspective soon."

Abby shook her head. "Nope, not going to happen. Life doesn't suck, I agree, but I'm not going to accept that I have to be limited. Neither should you. Has being legally blind stopped you, Sam, from living? From trying new things?"

Sam chuckled. "You've got me there. Fine. Tell you what. Why don't we plan a trip? Before your courses start. You can blog about the research and how best to pack, and then take as many photos for Instagram as you want. Okay? We can go someplace warm, where we can stick our toes in the sand and feel the heat of the sun on our skin. I'll have a week of vacation time in July."

"I don't want to wait until then," Abby said. She stared at the postcard, turning it over in her hands. "Besides, we're still on for our timeline, right? You're not backing out, are you?" she asked.

"No, I'm not backing out. You know that. Have you talked to your dad yet?" Sam asked.

"I did." Abby groaned. "I even tried to—"

"What are you looking at?"

Startled, Abby let go of the postcard and almost dropped her phone at the sound of her father's voice.

"Hey, is that your dad? Say hi for me."

"Sam says hi, Dad."

She loved the way her father's eyes lit up at the mention of Sam's name.

"Is she still planning on coming up this weekend?" he asked.

"What?" She didn't know that. "Truth, Sam? You're coming? Why didn't you say anything?" She loved having Sam come. It meant an end to her boredom.

"I was going to surprise you." Sam sighed rather dramatically. "Thanks, Josh."

"She says thanks for ruining her surprise, Dad." She winked.

"Sorry!" He held his hands up in mock surrender. "Do you have a moment or want to meet me downstairs in a bit?"

"Sam? I'll call you back." Without waiting for a response, she hung up. "What's up?" She hoped it was something good, like they were going out for dinner and then sipping hot chocolate after skating around the ice rink downtown.

"What's that in your hand?"

Abby noticed the way her father stood, arms crossed over his chest, leaning against the doorway without actually stepping into the room.

"One of Mom's postcards." She flipped it over. "I can't read who sent it to her though." She held it out and waited to see if he'd step in.

"I think that was from one of our readers. Your mom especially loved the ones from overseas." He just stood there, not coming in.

The silence between them grew for a moment. "Did she ever visit Germany and see the markets for herself?"

Her dad shook his head. He looked like he was about to say something then stopped. He walked away, heading back down the stairs.

Abby ran after him, stopping at the top and looking down.

"Dad? You wanted to talk to me?" she called out.

He hesitated and then turned, looking up at her.

"I'm sorry," she said. "I don't know what I did, but . . ." He looked as if she'd just broken his heart. How would mentioning Germany do that?

He shook his head. "No." He cleared his throat. "No, you didn't do anything. Come downstairs when you're ready. Dr. JJ called. She's on her way here."

Abby gripped the banister tight. "Did she say why she's coming?"

"She's bringing the family up to spend the weekend at their cottage. Her husband wants to do some ice fishing on the lake, and she has your results. Saves us a trip to the city." He swallowed hard.

"Did she say anything about them?"

He shook his head.

"No hint? Nothing?" Abby couldn't believe Dr. JJ would do that.

"She'll be here in an hour, after she drops off the kids and her husband at the cottage."

She could tell that he was making an effort to seem optimistic for her sake—he smiled but the visible tendons on his neck were a giveaway.

Abby ran down the stairs, almost plowing into her father and wrapped her arms around him. She knew he was worried that the results would come back showing there were no improvements. But she didn't feel the same. She remained positive and needed him to as well.

"You're the best dad ever. You know that, right?" She rested her cheek on his back.

"I'm the only one you've got, so of course I am."

There was a smile in his voice. She could hear it. She squeezed harder and then let her arms drop. "You're the only one *I've* ever needed." She waited till he turned around. "Dr. JJ coming here could only mean one thing, right?"

It took longer than she'd expected for him to nod.

Abby stopped herself from reminding her dad about all his lectures on staying positive, about focusing on the future, and not letting doubts and fears stop them from living a full life.

"I'm going to go bake them some cookies." Abby turned and headed into the kitchen. "Want to help?" It would keep him distracted until Dr. JJ showed up.

Her dad shook his head. "I'm going to go work on grading more papers. But I'll come down and taste test some if you want."

"Dad?" She called out as he climbed the stairs. "It's good news. I know it. I feel good, I really do."

He searched her face, as if looking behind her words. But, she was telling the truth. She felt fine.

Pneumonia wasn't fun, not with her lungs. And as much as she complained about not being able to go outside and enjoy the snow, she knew how important it was to avoid catching a cold. She knew that better than anyone.

Her last attack had been almost a year ago. She'd been in the hospital for a total of nineteen days and fourteen hours, hooked up to IV drips and beeping monitors that she swore she could still hear in her sleep. But since then, she'd been fine.

That was a word her father hated. *Fine.* "Use your words," he'd say to her over and over. He wanted her to describe how she actually felt rather than give a vague sense of wellness that might gloss over the truth. He used to tell her how her mom would tell him she was fine when she was anything but. He'd grown to cringe whenever she'd tell him that.

"Your words to God's ears, kiddo," her dad said before he continued up the stairs, his tread heavy as he made his way to his room.

"Please, God, let it be good news," she prayed softly. There was so much riding on this—both her freedom and her father's freedom from constantly worrying about her. He needed this to be good news as much as she did.

For the next hour, Abby baked a batch of homemade oatmeal chocolate chip cookies and even managed to whip up some cinnamon and sugar muffins, which she knew Dr. JJ and her family liked.

Abby and her dad kept to themselves as they waited for Dr. JJ. And by the time she arrived, they'd both been sitting silently in the living room, staring out the front window, in a holding pattern till they caught sight of her car.

When her dad opened the door, Abby didn't give her a chance to even set foot inside the house before she launched herself into her doctor's arms for a big hug.

"It's so good to see you," Abby said as she squeezed tight the woman who meant so much to her.

Dr. JJ was more than just her physician. She'd been a constant in Abby's life for as long as she could remember, always by her side when she was sick, a friendly face when she was worn down, a confidante when she felt lonely and isolated. Dr. JJ was family, *her* family, and regardless of what news she brought today, Abby was happy to see her.

"Whoa!" Dr. JJ laughed, kissed Abby on the cheek, and shrugged off her coat. "With a hug like that, I might start thinking you missed me." She handed the coat to Abby.

Abby's smile grew even wider. "Well, it has been"—she mentally counted the days since she'd last seen her—"fifteen days since we last had coffee together." She'd driven down to the city with her dad for her pulmonary function test and chest X-ray, but it had been a rushed visit, since her father had classes to teach the following morning.

"If Wade is looking for company, I could handle a day on the lake," her dad piped up while they all went into the kitchen, where a fresh pot of coffee waited. Without asking whether Dr. JJ wanted any, Abby poured her a cup and held out the plate of cookies.

"He thought you might say that. He said he'd text you some-time tonight. He's hoping you have an auger he can borrow?" She bit into one of the cookies and moaned. "So good," she said with her mouth full.

Abby listened to the inane conversation about ice fishing until she couldn't stand it.

"So, am I okay?" She blurted it out, completely interrupting them.

Dr. JJ set her coffee down and looked Abby straight in the eye.

"Your pulmonary function test results were good. The spirometry test looks encouraging and so does the plethysmography, where we measured the volume of gas in your lungs. Both are as close to normal as we've ever seen them, Abby."

The air sucked out of the room, leaving Abby breathless as the news sunk in.

"You're kidding, right?" The words rushed out.

"How about the chest X-rays?" her father questioned at the same time.

Dr. JJ gave a little shrug. "It's what we'd talked about previously. You're still at stage three in regards to the scarring, but the regeneration since your last bout of pneumonia is decent. Basically, your lungs are healing. Slower than I'd like, since it's been almost a year from the time you were last sick, but healing nonetheless."

Abby's throat tightened with emotion, and her eyes welled with tears. She gasped so deeply it brought on a coughing fit that led to her fiddling with her inhaler while Dr. JJ rubbed her back in small circles to calm her down. She needed to get the steroids into her lungs so she could breathe properly again.

She glanced up at her dad, who had tears in his eyes too.

"I'm okay. I'm really okay," Abby whispered.

"You're okay," her dad whispered back before enveloping both the doctor and Abby in a big bear hug.

"Whoa there," Dr. JJ said, as she pulled back. She put her hands on Abby's shoulders and let the weight of them sink in. "Not so fast. This doesn't mean you can go wild and crazy and go ice fishing with your father for hours on end or traipse around in the snow all day. Abby, your lungs are badly damaged, and you need to keep that in mind. There's still considerable risk of you getting sick, going back into the hospital, and before you know it, all the progress you've made this past year will be out the window." Dr. JJ's gaze rested intently on her face, and Abby had to look away.

"I mean it. You don't need to be holed up in the house, although I'm sure your father would prefer it, but—"

"I get it. I've got to be smart. I can go ice-skating at least, right? Have a snowball fight? Go for a walk and not worry that it's too much?" Abby asked.

"Strap on your skates. Have fun outside and get some light exercise, but be careful. Know your limits. Don't push it. If you find yourself reaching for your inhaler too often, then you know you've probably done too much. I've said it before, but I'll reiterate: a warm climate with moist air is the best thing for you. Why you're not in the Caribbean right now relaxing by the ocean is beyond me." She shook her head, but Abby could see her eyes twinkling.

Dr. JJ downed the last of her coffee and picked up the tin of cookies and muffins Abby had slid in front of her earlier. "Wade will love these," she said.

"They're for everyone, and I can make more to send with Dad tomorrow. Sam's coming for the weekend too, so I'll be making some of her favorites as well."

"Sam's coming? If I'd known that, I would have given her a ride. If the boys catch anything tomorrow, let's plan on dinner, okay?" With a wave, she let herself out, leaving them standing there in the kitchen, the import of her news slowly settling all the way in.

"I'm okay, Dad." Abby still could not believe it. She let out a long breath, grateful the heavy weight of fear she'd been carrying was dissipating.

Her dad nodded, and as he turned toward her, she watched the emotions sweep across his face. He pulled her in for a long hug, kissing the top of her head and refusing to let go.

She didn't mind. She'd always felt safe in her dad's arms, and she knew exactly what he was feeling.

For the first time in twenty years, they'd received unambiguously positive news. Her previous results were never this good.

It was like a dream come true, which scared her because her dreams had never come true before. Not like this.

FIVE

MILLIE

"Did you hear?" Abby opened the front door, her face beaming and her body vibrating with excitement.

"I heard, my girl. I heard." Millie couldn't contain the tears, hadn't been able to since Josh called them late last night to give her the scoop.

She'd sent off an e-mail straight away, ordering Abby's favorite cake from Sweet Bites Bakery, the family-run pastry shop in town.

"Want to go ice-skating with me?" Abby asked.

Millie laughed. "Girl, this old body doesn't belong on ice skates." She bit her lip when she saw the crestfallen look on her granddaughter's face. She patted Abby's cheek and smiled, eliciting a bright smile in return. "I know it's not as fun as ice-skating, but we brought cake." She stepped to the side and gave David room to come in. He was carrying the box from the bakery and presented it to Abby as he came forward.

"You're my favorite, you know that, right?" Abby grinned at Millie while she took the box from David's hands and then led them all into the kitchen.

"I'd better be your favorite," Millie teased. "I'm so happy, kiddo," she whispered, her voice catching in her throat. She didn't want to cry again. She'd done enough of it last night, enough to bring on a scathing headache.

"Every time I think about it—that I'm really okay—I just . . . it's overwhelming, you know?" Abby admitted as she opened the cake box. "I mean, I knew that it would be okay. I've had this feeling . . . but for it to be official, to hear Dr. JJ say it. It was almost too much. Does that make sense?"

Millie reached for David's hand and squeezed, unable to say the words she longed to.

"Makes perfect sense, Abby," David said. "Now's the time for us all to let out that collective breath we've been holding."

"I'm breathing," Abby said. "Trust me, I'm breathing. For the first time in a long time. And it's wonderful."

"Where's your father?" David asked.

"One of his students called a few minutes ago. He's upstairs in his office." Abby eyed the cake. "Do we have to wait for him? This looks delicious."

It was a French vanilla, three-layered cake with coconut cream between the tiers and chocolate–whipped cream frosting on top.

"Let's wait," Millie said. "Hopefully, he won't be too long. Besides, I have something to show you."

Abby's eyes lit up.

Millie was trying very hard to keep a lid on her excitement. She came up with an amazing idea last night, an idea that had been twenty years in the making.

"But first, tea," David said.

Millie caught his glance and knew he was trying to tell her to slow down and not rush this. She pressed her lips together to keep from smiling even more than she already was and fiddled with a tea towel that sat on the counter.

David had already turned on the kettle and prepared the teapot. He opened the container of tea that he'd given Abby for Christmas one year that had been full of peppermint, dried orange peel, chamomile, echinacea, and goji berries, herbs he believed would help boost her immune system.

"It's a good thing I brought a new blend." David held up the empty container.

"I totally forgot to mention I'd run out," Abby apologized. "Sorry."

"That's why I always come prepared." David winked at her.

"Keep drinking it, honey," Millie added.

"Yes, Grandma." Abby rolled her eyes.

"Don't get smart with me. How do you know it's not the tea David's been making for you that has kept you healthy?" Every so often, Millie liked to put her cheeky granddaughter in her place.

"She's a clever one, that grandma of yours," David teased as he refilled the container and then finished brewing their tea.

Millie smiled and giggled a little inside. Yes, it was definitely time.

"Come sit with me for a minute." She reached for Abby's hand and led her to the table. "I want to tell you a story."

She'd discussed this with David last night while in bed and then again this morning. She knew she might be overstepping a little, and, in truth, she was a tad worried about how Josh would react.

David had pointed out that it was going to be hard for everyone to let Abby grow up.

But Millie knew it was more than that. Abby was Josh's life. After Claire's death, and with Abby's illnesses, his sole focus was her, and only her. He gave up his writing career, teaching online courses for years so he could be available for his daughter, and only recently took the position at the local college teaching creative writing.

If any man was going to suffer an identity crisis, it was her son-in-law.

Abby had a hard time sitting down at the table with her. She couldn't get comfortable in her chair and jumped up a few times to add some cookies she'd made yesterday to a plate that was already full.

"Child, sit. You're making me dizzy." Millie tapped the tabletop with her hands. "You're reminding me of when you were little. You hated sitting still, wanting to flit around the room, getting overexcited until you couldn't breathe, and your father would have to hold you in his arms until you calmed down." She'd always been a child so full of energy.

Abby arched an eyebrow. "A story? Now?"

Millie sighed with obvious exasperation. "Yes, now. It's an important one, and one I've been wanting to tell you for years."

"It has a happy ending." David placed teacups in front of them, and then stood at the counter, observing with a watchful eye. "You're not going to wait for Josh?" he asked.

She wrinkled her nose at the idea. "I'm allowed to tell my grand-daughter a story without her father being around," she huffed.

"It's not the story I'm worried about," he reminded her.

"Life isn't all about happy endings. You guys know that, right?" Abby interjected. Abby raised her teacup and took a small sip.

Millie let hers sit there for a little bit. She preferred not to burn her tongue.

"Your mother liked the ones with happy endings, and this is a story about your mom."

That caught Abby's attention. "About my mom?"

Millie nodded. "One I've never told you, so listen up." She pulled out a notebook from her purse and set it down on the table.

"Is that one of my mom's journals?" Abby's eyes were glued to the book as she reached out to lightly touch it.

"From when she was younger. Your mother kept a journal since she was in the third grade. Back then, her entries were full of how her days went and what she did, but they eventually changed to lists, like the ones you already have of hers. This was probably one of her first lists. You have all her other ones, right?"

"Between my dad and me, we do. There are a few he hasn't let me read yet, though."

"Some are probably too personal," Millie said as she flipped the book open and looked through the pages at random. Claire had drawn pictures on a few—houses surrounded by fields of flowers, with some puppy dogs and unicorns too.

She kept turning the pages until she found the one she sought, one close to the end.

"Read this and tell me what catches your eye." She pushed the page closer to Abby and waited. She knew the list by heart, having looked through and read this journal many times throughout the years.

Claire's bucket list (age 13)

1. ~~Marry a man who loves me more than life itself and makes me laugh. And makes me cry, and then holds me as I'm crying and cries with me.~~
2. Learn to surf.
3. Speak Italian like a native.
4. Scuba dive the reefs of Australia.
5. ~~Learn to draw.~~
6. ~~Be an artist.~~
7. Go to Hawaii.
8. Be in a movie—even as an extra.
9. Meet someone famous and pretend it's no big deal.
10. See penguins in their natural habitat. *(But that would mean I'd have to go where it's cold—not sure I can do that.)*
11. Help build an orphanage in Africa.
12. Eat breakfast with Mickey and Minnie Mouse at Disney World, and take a graphic design lesson with a Disney illustrator. *(Wouldn't that be cool?)*

13. Be a mother.
14. ~~Travel.~~
15. Travel—everywhere. *(This can't ever be checked off. I'm sure there will always be places I want to explore.)*
16. ~~Learn to play the piano.~~
17. Skydive. *(I'm afraid of heights, but if my instructor were super cute, I could handle it.)*
18. See an actual fistfight or bar brawl as it happens. I always hear about it or read about it . . .
19. Tour Christmas markets in Germany, and eat all the gingerbread I want without getting into trouble for it!

Abby's smile grew increasingly bright as she quietly read her mother's list out loud. "It's nice to see that she crossed off number one on the list. She really loved my father, didn't she?"

"I wish you could have seen them together. Never have I seen a couple more perfect. They really did complete each other, for the better. Your father made your mom a better person. Just like"—Millie reached her hand out toward David—"this man here does for me. David has taught me what it means to be an equal in a relationship. When it came to your parents, there was never a question about them being a team, they just were."

Millie's heart almost burst with happiness as her husband gently kissed the top of her hand, his lips lingering a bit before he gave her a wink.

After her first disastrous marriage, she never imagined she'd find love, not like this. Not at her age.

Most of the women she'd grown up with were either dead or living in retirement homes, happy to play Scrabble or watch the news. They'd lived their lives and were just marking time until death.

Not her. Not David. She wanted to die in her sleep, wrapped up in the arms of the man who owned her heart.

"My mom always wanted to travel, didn't she?"

"She did. There were so many places she wanted to see. Did you know we had a trip planned, just the two of us?"

"Millie, maybe we should wait for Josh." David's voice was low, and she knew he was warning her to stop. She ignored him. Josh knew they were there. He could have ended his call early to come down and see them. It's not like she hadn't tipped him off that she was coming over with a surprise . . .

Abby leaned back in her chair and folded her arms. "What is going on?"

"Nothing," Millie said.

"So you had a trip planned with Mom? To where? How come this is the first I'm hearing about it?" Abby shot off her questions.

Millie pulled a letter from her purse. "How about I let your mom explain?"

She opened the letter and reread Claire's words silently before she cleared her throat. She looked up at her granddaughter for a moment, and then she focused on one specific paragraph.

I know I've been asking a lot of you in this letter, but I have one more request. When Abby is old enough, will you take her on our trip? The one we'd planned to take but never did? I wish it were you and I taking Abby together, a girls' trip to end all girls' trips, but I'd still like you to go, even if I'm not there to join you. Will you? Hopefully, Josh has already taken her on a lot of trips by the time you plan this one . . . Josh and I talked so much about the things we would like to do with our daughter, the places we would go, but this was never one that came up in our conversations. Probably because this

*trip was never about me and Josh. It was about us. Use
our account, Mom, the one we set up for our Christmas
shopping, the one we put money in every year so we could
take this trip together (I hope there is enough. If not, tell
Josh to pay the rest . . . tell him I said so. He never could
say no to me).*

Millie raised her gaze from the letter. "No truer words have ever
been written." She smiled.

*Enjoy the Christmas markets in Germany, Mom.
Find the best gingerbread cookie and drink the finest
gluhwein and savor every moment of the Christmas
experience there. Share my love of the season with my
daughter, in Germany.*

Millie set the letter down and waited while Abby processed what
she'd just heard.

"Germany? She wanted you to take me to Germany?" Abby said
in disbelief.

Millie nodded as her smile grew. "Let's celebrate your healthy
doctor's report. And what better way than a trip to Germany to walk
through all the Christmas markets."

"But . . . but . . . ," Abby sputtered, trying to take it all in. "Germany?"
She leaned back in her chair and clasped her hands together.

"What about Germany?" Josh entered the kitchen.

Millie swallowed, and her eyes slid over toward her husband.

Abby jumped out of her seat and went to Josh, hugging him hard
with irrepressible excitement.

"Millie's taking me to Germany." Abby pulled away, oblivious to
the tension in the room. "It's what Mom wanted." She reached for the
letter and held it up, waving it around.

Millie quickly snatched it back. There was more to the letter than just the part about this trip, and she didn't need Abby to read it. Or Josh.

"Excuse me?" Josh asked, his tone a tad bit . . . frosty.

Millie grimaced.

"It's an early Christmas and celebrating-her-health gift rolled into one," David said, jumping in. "She's been wanting—"

"I think Millie can speak for herself," Josh interrupted him.

"Now, wait here a minute," David said.

"Joshua—" Millie began, but Josh held his hand up for quiet, which stopped her.

The kitchen had gone dead silent as everyone waited for what Josh would say.

"I'm sure I heard Abby wrong—right?"

"Joshua, you heard her right. I was just breaking the news to Abby. It's a surprise."

"A surprise?"

"This is something Claire and I had planned for years, and now seems like the time to finally go." She tried to sound nonchalant.

Josh's eyebrows rose almost to his hairline. "Claire's not here, and I don't remember you talking to me about taking a European trip in the middle of winter with Abby." His arms crossed over his chest.

"That's because I haven't yet. The idea occurred to me last night, after you called me. I bought the tickets this morning." She knew this would be a tough sell, but she wasn't backing down.

"You bought . . . ," he stammered.

"You heard me correctly."

"Without asking me first?" Josh's face reddened.

"I want to take my granddaughter on a trip."

"Yeah, I kind of got that." A vein in his neck twitched.

"Don't be like this, Dad," Abby interjected. She rose from her seat and went over to her father, reaching out for his hands. "I'm an adult, not a child anymore, and Dr. JJ herself said I was okay."

"So you're in on this?" he asked her.

Abby shook her head. "Didn't you hear Millie? It was a surprise. Why are you so upset?" Abby pulled her hands back and wrapped her arms around her body as if protecting herself from him.

Millie didn't like that at all.

"Josh, we don't need to get upset. I just—"

"You just what?" He spat the words out. "Just thought to take my daughter away from me? Take her halfway across the world, in the middle of winter on some dream trip you've never bothered to tell me about?" He stepped forward into Millie's personal space. David shoved his arm between them, preventing Josh from getting any closer.

Josh backed up a step and stuck his hands in his jean pockets, but the anger was still there. Millie could see it in the creased lines between his eyebrows.

"Dad?" Confusion steeped Abby's voice, and for a moment, Millie worried he wasn't going to hear it.

Josh's head dropped until his chin almost hit his chest and his shoulders bowed in.

"I'm sorry, Abs. I really am. That was . . . uncalled for." He lifted his head and looked at his daughter.

"You should apologize to Millie too," Abby whispered.

Josh let out one long breath before he looked at David and Millie.

"You know I've always wanted to travel." Abby laid her hand on her father's arm. "This is such a great surprise and a perfect way to celebrate my clean bill of health, isn't it? If Dr. JJ is okay with it, why can't you be?" Abby swallowed, stealing a glance at Millie before standing in front of Josh. She whispered, "Please?"

Millie couldn't see the look on her granddaughter's face, but the pleading in her tone almost broke her heart.

She'd expected Josh to be upset, but not like this.

"No."

Suddenly exhausted, Millie slumped back in her chair and went to pick up her teacup, but stopped as she noticed her hands shaking.

"A trip sounds like a wonderful idea." Josh cleared his throat. "But why halfway across the world? What about some of the other things you've talked about doing? Like a beach vacation or spending Christmas at Disney World?" he suggested, his voice now mellow, almost apologetic.

"Or the Christmas markets in Germany like Mom always wanted to do?" Abby said softly. "It's on her list, you know? And she wrote it in a letter, asking Millie to take me." She placed her arms around her father, and Millie looked away, feeling more than just defeated.

She felt old. Ancient. Weary and worn. She'd been so excited when she first thought of this, but maybe she had waited too long. Too long for this dream to come true. She should have gone to Germany all those years ago with David, when he'd first suggested it to her. *Silly me,* she thought. She'd held out, wanting to honor her daughter's wishes, and had waited for Abby to be well enough to go.

The reality was that she was getting too old to travel the world as she'd always wanted to. Going to Germany wasn't necessary. They could still do a trip, but something like what Josh had mentioned. Maybe a cruise would work.

"If you want to go so badly, why don't you two go?" Josh asked David and Millie, a tortured look in his gaze.

"I can't go right now," David answered. "And I really don't want Millie going by herself, and let's face it"—he gave her an apologetic look—"we don't have so many years left in us that traveling alone makes sense."

"Dad, why don't you come too? We don't have to do a lot. If we stay in the Bavaria region, we can do Munich and Nuremberg and . . . Oh, we could go to Salzburg too, since it's so close by train." Abby stopped abruptly and bit her lip.

Millie leaned forward in her chair. "You've been researching the markets, and the cities and sights?"

Abby gave a small nod. "I was looking at the postcards in Mom's office, and then I told Sam about it."

Millie chuckled. "You're so much like your mother," she said wistfully. "Claire was always planning a trip, wasn't she?" Her smile faded as she caught Josh's reaction.

His eyes grew round as he looked from his daughter to Millie. His mouth opened and closed, as if unsure of what to say, but it was the look in his eyes that hit Millie hard.

Panic. Pure panic, which he was desperately trying to hide from his daughter.

"Now, as much as I'd love to traipse around Germany"—David cleared his throat—"I think this is a girls-only trip."

Abby turned and said, "But we can make it a family trip, right Millie?"

Josh slowly shook his head behind Abby's back.

"Well, I . . ." She hated saying no to her girl, but this was something Josh was going to have to deal with on his own. "I was really hoping it could be just us, love. Besides, I only booked two tickets, and your father still has classes, don't you, Josh? Maybe . . ." She caught the disappointment on Abby's face and paused for a breath. "Maybe they could join us later? We could always change our return flight." She smiled weakly at Abby and then at Josh, who abruptly turned and left the room.

"I just need a moment," he said as he ran down the hallway. In the silence that followed him, the tiny click of the bathroom door closing could be heard distinctly.

"What . . . is he okay?" Abby looked lost, almost helpless, as she stood in the doorway and stared down the hall after her father.

"Well now. You know how much your father hates surprises," David said kindly, "and this, well, this one was a doozy." He gave Millie a look, one she could read like a highway sign.

"I didn't handle this properly." She sighed and sat back down. "I'll apologize when he returns."

"For what?" Abby sipped at her tea. "I am an adult, remember? You didn't need to ask his permission, if that's what you're going to apologize for."

Millie shook her head. For all the bravado in Abby's words, her voice wavered, giving away her genuine disquiet about her father. Millie glanced at David. He gave a quick nod back.

"I'll go see if he's okay," he said and left the kitchen.

Millie reached out for Abby's hands, holding them tight between her own. "Yes, you're an adult, but to your father, you're still his little girl. You know that." She smiled warmly. "For twenty years, he's been by your side, taking care of you, worrying over you. I've never known a man to be so dedicated to his family as your father. You are his everything, honey."

"But I shouldn't be. Not anymore. He needs a life of his own, a life that doesn't revolve around me or my health—right? I want my own life, Millie."

"I know you do." Millie agreed with her. But, sometimes life wasn't so clear, the lines weren't always so straight when it came to what should happen and what did happen. "Have patience. I know you've probably been planning this day for years—the day you're given the green light, that you're healthy enough to live your own life without being cooped up in this house—but your father, he probably never thought this day would come. Or if he did, he didn't believe it, not really."

"Well, he should have," Abby said quietly. "I know he always thought he'd lose me, like he did Mom, but he hasn't yet."

"Nor will he," Millie said. She believed that with all her heart. "But you need to give him time to adjust. And me springing this trip on him—well, that was me not giving him time." She sighed. "David did warn me."

The corner of Abby lips twitched until a smile appeared. "I can't believe you did this. And you really bought the tickets already?"

Millie nodded. "I figured he wouldn't say no if he knew I'd already spent the money." She winked.

"When do we leave?" Excitement lit up Abby's features.

"Your passport is up to date, right?"

"I renewed it two years ago when we crossed the border and went shopping in Arizona, remember?"

Millie nodded. That's what she thought.

"How does four days from now sound?"

Abby gasped. "Four days?" She coughed as her breath snagged, but as soon as she could breathe again, she giggled like the happy child Millie remembered with fondness. "Are you serious?" Abby asked. Her eyes widened into huge *O*'s until her whole face beamed.

Millie loved that reaction. "I'm totally serious. I thought we could stop in London first and visit the little bed-and-breakfast your parents stayed at while they were there. It's in that book your mom made you, right?"

Abby grinned with delight.

"Now," Millie continued, "four days doesn't leave us much time, but I figured you could help me research hotels, and of course, you'll want to blog about all that. Plus Sam is coming tonight, and I didn't want to ruin your time with her."

"We're actually leaving in a few days? That's pure craziness!"

That's exactly what David had said until Justyna, David's niece, who was a travel agent, found a good deal for them this morning—too good to pass up. She had also recommended a tour guide she'd booked previously for other clients. Millie hadn't wanted to use a guide, quite happy to plan the itinerary herself, until David gave her a look that told her she either hired the guide or didn't go. It was amazing how easy it was to read his facial expressions. Given that and Justyna's glowing endorsement of the tour guide, and the reasoning that it would make for a stress-free travel experience, Millie acquiesced with only a little more fuss. She was all for reducing stress, and she had a suspicion that a guide might help alleviate Josh's anxieties as well, which couldn't hurt.

"How long do you need to plan a trip you've been waiting your whole life for?" Millie asked.

SIX

ABBY

Abby's Journey: A Personal Blog

Best. Day. Ever!

You read that right. Today is the best day ever! Not only did I get my one-year clean bill of health (can we say It's. About. Time!!!) but I'm going to Germany!

You read that right. I—Abigail Turner, the girl who has been dreaming of traveling her whole life—finally get to live my dreams. In the middle of winter! My grandmother and I are headed to Germany for a Market tour ... yep ... outdoor, mittens-required, hot-chocolate-drinking type markets. In. Germany!

(Insert smiling face here ... which is fairly accurate since I can Not. Stop. Smiling!) Off

to research the best markets and hotels in Munich . . . so much to do in so little time.

PS. If you've been to Munich, where did you stay? What's the one thing you'd recommend we do while we're there? I'm creating a list (of course).

"You're kidding me, right?" Sam shouted, her voice filling up the room.

Abby bounced in her chair. She couldn't help it.

"I know, right?" She had the speakerphone turned up as loud as possible in her mom's office. She stared at the wall full of postcards and giggled with glee.

She couldn't believe her dreams were coming true!

"Your grandma is the best, you know that? Mine just knits me scratchy sweaters." Sam had her on speakerphone as well, and she heard Dean, Sam's boyfriend, chuckle in the background.

It was true. Millie was awesome. Millie was more than just her grandmother. She was also her mother and friend. Millie was the constant, nurturing mother figure Abby had always known and depended on.

"You know what's so weird about all of this?" Abby twirled a length of hair in her fingers as she continued to gaze at the wall.

"What's that?" Sam asked.

"Just yesterday I said to you that I wanted to go to Germany. It's like Millie read my mind." She had been more than a little shocked earlier, when Millie broke the news. She was still trying to process it all. She was *actually* going to Europe.

Sam gasped. "That's right. I totally didn't think about that. It's so cool, Abby. So is it all booked? Like everything? Where are you staying? How long will you be there? Where exactly will you go?"

"We leave in four days, and only the flight is booked. Millie said something about using a tour company to take us around," Abby said.

"Four days?" Dean shouted.

"Four days!" Abby couldn't believe it.

"Tour company? Why not just do it yourself? Backpack across Germany . . . sounds like fun to me," Dean added.

"I doubt her grandmother wants to backpack," Sam replied.

"I guess."

"When will you get here?" Abby asked. She couldn't wait to see Sam. It had been way too long.

"We're an hour away," Dean said.

"Can you stay for dinner, Dean, or are you wanting to see your parents right away? I know you prefer pie, but will cake do?" She liked Dean. She liked to tease them that they were the perfect *Supernatural* fan couple, and they had the names to prove it. It was too bad Sam hadn't named her dog Castiel.

At the word *cake,* Abby heard Dean practically purring in the background.

"You just said the magic word," Sam said with a giggle. "We'd better call his parents, and let them know he'll be late. See you soon, girl!"

Abby's eyes glided over the wall of postcards in her mother's study, and a wave of giddiness washed over her.

"I'm going to Germany, Mom. Just like you wanted," she said quietly.

She thought about all the journals she'd read of her mother's, all the notes she'd read, the things she'd been told. She tried to place herself in her mom's shoes—what would she do right now after deciding to take a trip? What had she done in the past?

One look at the bookshelf behind her and Abby knew.

There was one section of the shelf that was Abby's. Her mother had bought a few dozen blank journals, all different colors and sizes, and left them there for Abby to use. Most were now full. Since the age of ten, Abby had kept her own yearly journals, but they weren't exciting ones, full of wishes and dreams and hopes for the future, not like her mother's.

Abby's were daily accounts of what her life was like as a sick child. Most of her entries were during hospital stays, describing how she felt and what she did to keep herself occupied.

There was one thing, however, in each of her journals that was like something her mother would do. She would save a few pages at the back of the book, and record her hopes and dreams. They weren't long-term ones—like who she would marry or what her career would look like—instead they were annual goals, what she wanted to accomplish that year. Most were repeats from the previous year, things she'd never been able to do, like learn to ski or ice-skate on a real pond rather than at an indoor rink at the mall. She wrote about wishing to be healthy for Christmas or going a full month without any hospital visits.

There was also one entry that would never change.

Use my passport to travel to someplace new.

It wasn't as though her father had never taken her anywhere. One summer, over a long weekend, they'd driven down to Stowe, Vermont, and camped in Derek and Abigail's large camper—and she wasn't sick. But they would never go anywhere far, just in case. Her dad would never take the chance.

She really couldn't blame him. She was sick a lot as a child and young teen.

There was one notebook on the shelf she'd never touched. The book had a cork cover with the words *Travel Journal* stamped on the spine and front cover. Inside, a special note had been written, one Abby knew by heart.

She reached for the journal and held it tight to her chest.

My dear sweet Abby,

I've always kept a travel journal, where I'd plan all my trips—real or imagined. Those journals are full of hotel names, tours, places to see, top ten lists for different countries or cities . . . all the things I would look into when planning my journeys.

I hope you'll use this likewise. Write down everything—all the things you research and find, places to visit, and tours to take. Don't always stick to the obvious tourist things either—be willing to take the back roads, see the sights only locals know about. Read travel magazines and websites, buy books, and look at pictures. Create your own unique trip, one that will forever be meaningful to you! But most of all, have fun planning your excursions. For me, that's the part I enjoy the most . . . the anticipation of the journey. You don't always need an agenda, but you should never be bored either. Enjoy life to the fullest, Abby, and you can never go wrong.

I love you. Happy travels.

Mom

Abby took the journal to her mother's desk and sat. She opened the journal and creased the spine. At the top of the first page, she wrote the word *Germany.* She then turned on the laptop, pulling her legs beneath her, and began searching for Christmas markets in Germany. She first did a search for the top ten markets and found multiple lists. She started to write down the names that showed up most often, along with the dates and times the markets were open.

She discovered that some markets ran daily while others were only open on weekends or for specifics weeks. A few, like Salzburg, Austria, were even open after Christmas.

She drew a star beside Salzburg. Even though it wasn't a German market, it was still reviewed as one of the best markets to visit and was only a two-hour train ride from Munich. Hopefully, she could convince Millie to go.

The more she read, the more she couldn't believe they were doing this. She was doing this.

It was a dream come true.

"You look so much like your mother right now."

Abby looked up and smiled at her father.

"You can come in, you know," she said.

He just stood there, at the edge of the room, arms folded over his chest as he leaned against the doorframe.

"Preparing for your trip?" he asked.

Abby nodded. It had taken a lot to get her dad to back down and accept the fact she was going on this trip. She'd never stood up to him like that before, but this was too important to her for her to concede. She'd thought long and hard about all of this—about her dad and his response. He was afraid, and she knew that, but she wasn't about to let his fear dictate the limits on her life, not when the fear was his and his alone.

"I want to make sure it's the best trip of my life, you know?" She held his gaze, determined to get him to fully comprehend she was going to go, that she was an adult, that she was capable of making her own decisions.

"About that." He cleared his throat as he glanced away.

Abby pushed her chair away from the desk and stood. "No you don't. You're not allowed to do this."

"Do what?"

Abby stood in front of her father, her own arms crossed tight over her chest, and she frowned. "This. You will not do this, not now." She knew exactly what he was going to do—try to tell her she shouldn't or couldn't go. But that wasn't going to happen. Not this time.

"Aunt Abigail can give me a checkup before I leave, to give you peace of mind, but if Dr. JJ said I'm all clear, then you can't keep me here, Dad." How many times would she need to remind him she was an adult?

"I just want to protect you, Abby." There was a pained look in his eyes, making her feel guilty.

She reached forward and wrapped her arms around him in a hug. "I know," she said. "But you're going to have to let me go sometime. You know that, right?"

"That doesn't have to be today, though. I'm not ready." He squeezed her tight.

Abby sighed. Why did she have a feeling he'd never be ready?

"I think I talked Dean into staying for dinner when he drops Sam off." She pulled away from his hold. "I mentioned cake, which seemed to have won him over." She was deliberately avoiding his comment. She wanted to talk with Sam about their plan, and see if she had any good ideas on how to get her dad to relax. She hadn't brought up her moving—not since Millie dropped her bombshell.

"He's welcome anytime."

"Oh really?" Abby smiled. "So . . . ," she teased. "If I suggested he stay the night with Sam being here . . ." She knew exactly how he was going to react.

"Don't push it." Her father grimaced. "She's still a young girl to me, like you."

Abby burst out laughing. "She's almost thirty, Dad."

"You'll always be my little girl. Which brings us back to the reason I'm here."

Abby turned and leaned back against the desk, her hands gripping the edge.

"Germany," they said in unison.

"Try to understand—"

"I do." She stopped him. "I understand you want to protect me, and you want me to be healthy. Trust me, Dad, I want that too. Being sick, it's not who I am, and yet, it's who I've been my whole life. I want something more, Dad . . . I need to be someone more." She needed him to get that, to get her.

"Do you need to travel halfway across the world, during winter, to do that?"

She nodded slowly, her gaze resting steadily on him.

She watched as her father struggled to accept what she was saying, and she realized he couldn't.

Before either one could say another word, the doorbell rang. Abby glanced at her watch, puzzled. Sam was still about a half hour away.

"That's for you."

"For me?" She stepped past him and stood at the top of the stairs.

"Hello!" A voice rang out.

"Aunt Abigail!" Abby ran down the stairs. "Did you hear about the results?"

"Did we hear? What kind of question is that! I would hope we were your father's first phone call right after sharing the news with you." Derek followed Abigail in the door and wrapped his arms around Abby, lifting her off her feet in a hug. "We're so happy for you, sweetheart."

"Put her down, Derek. She's not a small child anymore." Abigail swatted his arm.

"Can I help it that I'm excited for her?" Derek ruffled the hair on Abby's head and then winked. "Besides, she'll always be my little Abby."

"Hello? When will you guys realize I'm a grown woman now?" She cast a glance up the stairs, where her father stood shaking his head.

Abigail gave her a side hug. "Sweetie, you could be old and gray, and they'd still think of you as their little girl. Just ignore them."

"Is that what you do? Ignore them?" Abby teased her aunt.

Derek rolled his eyes. "She perfected that art mere months after we married."

"Months *after?*" her father piped up. "I thought she learned that trick while you two were still dating."

"Enough, you two. Abby, I hope you've got your winter gear ready." Abigail's eyes twinkled, which piqued Abby's curiosity.

"Winter gear? Such as . . . ?"

"Mitts, hat, scarf, and boots. Enough clothing to stay warm, but no promises about remaining dry," Derek teased.

A huge smiled filled Abby's face.

"Today is officially considered a snow day, so come on, girl, let's go out and play."

For the next thirty minutes, Abby had the time of her life. She and her aunt made a family of snowmen, while her dad and Derek built a fort. All they needed was for Sam and Dean to arrive and the snowball fight could begin.

A familiar ache, like a ten-pound baby sitting on her chest, settled over Abby when she saw Sam and Dean pull up. Specks, Sam's chocolate lab guide dog, jumped out of the car. Dean waved at Abby and then went around to open Sam's door, gently kissing her before stepping back to let her out.

One day. One day she'd find a love like that.

"Sam!" Abby called out as she ran over to her friend.

"Look at you. You're so beautiful." Sam's hands went up to Abby's face. Her fingers danced along the skin, mapping Abby's cheekbones and smile, and then she enveloped her friend in a fierce hug.

"Are you ready for a snowball fight, Sam?" Abby's dad came over and wrapped his arms around them both, squeezing hard. "Boys against the girls, and the losers are in charge of snacks for the night."

"Oh, now that's not fair. Who asks the blind girl to the snowball fight?" Sam joked. "Besides, you tend to burn the popcorn every time I'm here."

"Smart aleck." Her dad rubbed the top of Sam's head and then slapped Dean on the back. "That girl of yours has a wicked arm, in case you haven't noticed."

"Oh, I've noticed." Dean smiled down at Sam, and Abby's heart swelled to see the love in the way they looked at each other.

"You're happy." Sam leaned close, her nose inches away from Abby's, eyes widened as she searched for signs of something not there. "Having fun?"

At the word *fun,* Specks started barking and running in a circle, chasing her tail. *Fun* was a command word for the dog to relax and play, and play was something Specks loved to do.

Abby laughed at the dog, laughed with Sam and Dean . . . she just let go and laughed. Her fingers were freezing, her mittens drenched by melted snow, her cheeks were no doubt bright red, and she couldn't feel her nose. But she'd never felt more alive.

"The time of my life. Come on, I need some help finishing up my snow family. There's something not quite right about them." She led Sam over to where she'd been building the snowmen.

"Other than being a tad bit lopsided, I think they're fine." Sam shrugged after she crouched down to study the snowmen.

"So says the blind woman." Dean laughed.

Sam stood and turned on the balls of her feet. Her lips quirked as she stared into her boyfriend's face, and then she leaned in to give him a kiss.

"A blind woman who will whoop your ass when we start the snowball fight." Sam gave a little hoot, as her eyebrows rose.

"Oh-ho!" Derek bellowed. "Listen to them fightin' words. Sounds like it's time to get this party started." He rubbed his hands together in anticipation.

"Are you ready, Abby?" her dad asked. Even he looked excited, which she hadn't seen in him for a very long time.

"Bring it, Dad. I've got a hankering for some caramel popcorn, though there's nothing worse than when you burn the kernels," she taunted.

Abby swiveled and bent down to put some finishing touches on one of the snow babies she'd built when she got smacked in the back with something hard. She toppled forward and squashed her snow baby.

"What's up with that?" she said when she'd regained her feet and turned around.

Her father stood there, a wicked grin on his face as he held a snowball in his hand.

"That was so not fair, Dad!" Abby hustled to pack her own snowball to return fire, but she was too late. His arm was already poised to throw another one.

Abby jumped up, shrieked, and ran for cover behind one of the forts the men had built earlier.

Let the snowball fight begin.

SEVEN

CLAIRE

To be read during the hard days.

> *Dear Josh,*
>
> *You are an amazing father. I've always known you would be.*
>
> *I also know that you'll probably have days when you doubt yourself. You've always been there for me on those days, when I wasn't sure I was enough, so let me be there for you now. I don't know what you're going through, but I do know one thing:*
>
> *You've got this.*
>
> *No matter what* this *is, you've got it.*
>
> *You can handle this, see it through, and come out stronger than before.*
>
> *You are an amazing father, Joshua Turner, and I have faith in you.*
>
> *I'm sorry I'm not here. It wasn't an easy decision, to put off treatment as long as I could, and if you're reading this, I obviously waited too long. I can't apologize enough for that . . . this was never the outcome I wanted.*

It should be the two of us together, weathering whatever storms come our way—as it has always been. I try not to think about what could go wrong. I can't fathom the thought of my death, of not helping you raise our daughter, of not having the chance to love you forever.

It's okay to be angry with me. To want to hate me. To be mad that I made the decision to make someone else more important than myself. But, how could I not, when you did that every day we've been together? You have loved me well, Josh. Loved me completely. It's because of that love that I was able to love our child with everything within me.

I hope one day you can forgive me for that.

Now, about our daughter. Be her Superman, her Captain America, or better yet, her Tony Stark. Live outside the box, parent the way only you can. Be the dad she knows you are, the dad she needs you to be. Be the man that other men in her life have to try to live up to, the one that no one else can ever live up to in her eyes. I never had a father like that, but I'm so glad our daughter does.

(Read this as often as you need to. I hope you never will. I hope nothing ever comes your way that makes you think for even one moment that you can't handle it. But we all know how fair life is. It's not. So just in case . . .)

I love you. Forever and always,

Claire

EIGHT

ABBY

Abby's Journey: A Personal Blog

Girlfriends Are the Best

I have the best friend a girl could ever ask for. My mom wrote me a letter once about having girlfriends, those who love you no matter what, who know you inside and out, who will let you get away with the little things because she sees the big picture. My mom stressed that it wasn't just important to have that type of friend, but to be that friend as well.

I bet she never thought that the little girl she'd met all those years ago at a bookstore would be my best friend now. But she's probably smiling as she watches us staying up till the wee hours of the morning sharing secrets.

I don't have a mom who is there to get to know my friends, who can help me figure out who to bring in close to my heart and who to keep at arm's length. I wish I did, I really do. But what I do have is a mom who brought the type of friend I need into my life—even though it wasn't on purpose—and I'm so thankful that she is always there for me, taking care of me.

Do you have that type of friend? Don't tell me their name, just tell me what they're like and why they're so special.

PS. You're all jealous of my friend, aren't you? You should be—she's awesome. So awesome that she brings me chocolate every time she comes to visit. And I love her so much that I don't complain when half the box is empty. LOL.

Abby sat cross-legged on the couch while Sam lounged comfortably in the corner chair, where she normally liked to sit and read. Both held a fresh cup of coffee in their hands, care of her father who'd been kind enough to make them breakfast before heading into town for a few hours.

"I've been thinking," Sam said.

"Should I be worried?" Abby teased.

"Behave yourself." Sam held Abby's favorite childhood book, *Wherever We Go*, the one her mother had both written and illustrated, not long before she died.

"Sorry." Abby took a sip of her coffee before giving Sam her full attention. "You were saying?"

"Do you remember when you used to talk about going to these places?" Sam held up the storybook featuring a little girl, aptly named Abby, and her adventures in Europe. "What if . . ." Sam stopped, thinking over her words. But she didn't need to continue. The same idea had niggled at Abby all night.

"What if"—Abby finished for her—"*I* went to these places? That's what you were going to suggest."

Sam nodded. "You've thought about it then?"

"I have. For years, actually. I think it's what she intended. I'd love to visit every place my mother ever wrote about, to see it through her eyes."

"Is there time though? You're not overseas for very long."

Abby frowned. "True. I know we're going to London, and I think Millie mentioned adding Belgium to the itinerary along with Munich." She scrunched her nose. "Guess it means I'll have to take another trip." She smiled at the idea, loving the fact that she could not just dream about this but she could actually do it. If she remained healthy, there was nothing stopping her from planning another trip to Italy and touring it, as her parents had before she was born.

Sam sighed and stretched. "I wish I could come with you."

"Could you?" Abby loved that idea and knew Millie would have no problem with it.

Sam frowned. "There's no way. I don't have enough vacation time or enough funds. I'll just have to go another time. Maybe we could go together, or I can talk Dean into planning a honeymoon in Europe."

"Are you sure? I could talk to Millie and—"

Sam shook her head, stopping Abby from saying more.

"I'm sure." Sam stood in front of her chair, and then bent forward at the hips, touching the tips of her fingers to her toes and letting out a soft groan. She maintained her pose for a few minutes before slowly straightening up again.

"Have you tried yoga yet?" Sam asked. "You really should."

Abby shook her head. "No, I haven't tried yoga yet. You realize you ask me that almost every time I see you?"

"I do? *Hmm.* Maybe one day you'll give me a different answer." Sam sat back down and flexed her feet. "So?" she prodded.

"Do you think the hotels from the book would still be around? That was twenty years ago." Part of her didn't want to hope that they would be. She remembered once when she was younger asking her dad whether he'd ever want to revisit those places.

His response had shocked her.

His face had paled before he shook his head no. "No doubt they're all closed or sold, and it wouldn't be the same. It would never be the same. Sometimes"—his voice hitched—"sometimes you can't go back."

She remembered the heavy, dense feeling of sadness that settled between them as he'd said those words, as if there was something he wasn't telling her, something that might hurt her as much as it was obviously hurting him.

She'd asked him what was wrong, but he'd only walked away and locked himself in his room for a while.

She never asked him again after that.

"Why not?" Sam said, pulling her back into the present and away from the memory. "If I remember correctly, the places where your parents loved to stay were bed-and-breakfasts or family-run hotels, right? Twenty years isn't that long, especially if the business stays in the family. A quick search online should tell you. You could always just ask your dad too. I think he's still in touch with a few of them, right? You still get birthday cards from that family in Italy?"

"Miima and Rocco? I do." Abby leaned over and pulled open a drawer, where she rummaged a bit before pulling out a card. Miima liked to draw scenes of the Amalfi coast on card stock and send them to her. Her dad thought it was Miima's way of enticing her to come for a visit. "This was the latest one." She opened it and read the words written inside. Her Italian wasn't the greatest, but she'd taken some courses and really enjoyed it when Miima wrote to her in Italian.

> *"Dolcissima Abby,*
> *Devi venire a vedere questo panorama di persona, in*
> *primavera è di un fascino intrigante. T'innamorerai*
> *dell'Italia e non vorrai più partire."*

"You do realize I don't understand Italian?" Sam tilted her head at her.

"This is rough, but, 'Sweetest Abby, you must come and see this . . .'—*view,* I think—'in person. It has an intriguing charm in the spring. You'll fall in love with Italy, and you'll never want to leave.'"

"That's it." Sam sighed wistfully. "You have to go. You've worked so hard on learning the language, you have to put it to use."

"I know, right?"

Sam reached for her coffee. "You never know, you might be able to talk your dad into going with you."

There was a change in Sam's voice that seized Abby's attention, and she lifted her gaze from her cup of coffee.

"Do you think he will?"

Sam shrugged. "Your dad is a lot stronger than he gives himself credit for. I think it'll take a bit but—"

"Do you think he'll try to stop me from going?" Abby interrupted Sam. It was something that had run through her mind all night—what if . . . what if he really pulled out all the stops and asked her not to go . . . for his sake.

If he said no from a place of authority, that was one thing. She would try to talk him out of it, as she'd already been doing.

But if he asked as a personal favor from the heart? He'd done so much for her, sacrificed so much—she didn't think she could say no to him if he put it like that.

"I think if he were going to, he would have by now. Your dad . . . he has a hard time letting you out of his sight."

Abby rolled her eyes. "Tell me about it."

"Baby steps, Abby. Take baby steps when it comes to your dad."

"If you're telling me not to go on this trip . . ." Sam wouldn't do that, would she? She wouldn't side with her father in this. She couldn't. At the thought of it, Abby's heart quickened for a beat, and the sudden, fierce squeeze sparked a sharp pain in her chest.

Sam shook her head. "No, honey." Sam came over and sat beside her on the couch, reaching across and touching her knee. "That's not what I'm saying. I think you should go—it's a dream come true and so special that it's Millie taking you. But maybe we should hold off on the other."

Hold off on their moving in together? How could she suggest that?

Abby sighed, suddenly feeling very discouraged. "Not fair, Sam. We've been planning this for months."

"A few more months won't hurt."

Abby tightened her lips and huffed. "A few more months could lead to six or nine or never. Dean won't want to wait forever, and eventually you'll realize that you don't need that level of independence before you marry him."

"A few months won't make that much of a difference, Abby. You know that." Sam lifted her chin, and she pulled back.

Instant regret ate away at the inside of Abby's heart. "I'm sorry. I'm acting like a—"

"Like a spoiled little brat who's only thinking of herself?" Then Sam said softly, "Except we both know that's not the truth." Sam directed her gaze toward the window. She got up and went to stand in front of it, her arms wrapped around herself.

"You're only twenty, Abby. I know you feel like life is rushing by you, but it's not. Trust me."

"Sam, are you okay?" The tone of her friend's voice, the way she stood at the window . . . it worried Abby.

"I'm fine, just a little melancholy when I think about our lives. When I was twenty, I had no idea what I wanted to do with my life. I was happy being at home with my parents. But you, you're ready to get out of your comfort zone, aren't you? Ready to grab onto life and savor every moment of the journey." Sam turned, a soft smile on her face. "I envy you, you know?"

Abby didn't say anything as Sam went back to sit beside her on the couch.

"I don't mean to sound ungrateful." Abby laid her head on Sam's shoulder.

"Then don't."

Two simple little words that said so much.

"You've got a father who worships the ground you walk on, who has fought for you every day of his life and will continue fighting for you even when you'd rather learn to stand on your own two feet. You should feel lucky and loved and . . ." Sam's voice caught in her throat.

"I do," Abby said.

Sam's father had recently passed away, and Abby had no doubt that pain would never cease.

She should know. She still mourned for a mother she never got to know.

They sat there like that for a few minutes before Sam patted her hand. "All right. We're wasting the day away with our laziness." Sam jumped up from the couch, and Specks sat at attention. "Because, hello? It's winter, and you're not locked away in this house or sick in a hospital bed. Want to go for a walk?"

Abby inhaled a rush of air, almost choking on it in her excitement. "Yes, let's! How about we walk down to our neighbor's house and give them a tin of cookies." They were an elderly couple and didn't get out too much anymore.

Sam started to chuckle.

"What's so funny?" Abby asked.

"We'd better make another batch or two then. I sneaked down in the middle of the night for a glass of water and noticed there were only a few cookies left."

Abby groaned. She knew she should have put some away, especially after Derek warned her she hadn't made enough. She should have known better.

"How many are a few?"

Sam shrugged. "I'm blind, remember?"

Abby snorted. "Flimsy excuse. How many did you eat while grabbing your glass of water?"

"One or two." A large grin graced Sam's face. She took a few steps back until she bumped the door. "How about I take a shower first? While you drink another cup of coffee. If you can get out all the ingredients, I'll start on a new batch of cookie dough."

"I'm not sure I trust you in the kitchen. Remember the last time you tried to bake? It was brownies or something, wasn't it? I seem to recall you mixing up a few of the ingredients and then actually burning them too," Abby teased. "Go have your shower. I'm going to start researching for the trip, and then maybe we can make the cookies together." While Sam showered, she'd do a little searching to see if that place in London was still open.

She was almost giddy with excitement.

She was going to Europe. Her stomach flipped in rhythm to the beat of her heart as the realization hit her once again.

As the screen loaded, Abby opened up the book her mother had written for her and flipped to the pages set in London. The little bed-and-breakfast in South Kensington was called Blossom Lane.

The image her mother had drawn was of a quaint two-level cottage surrounded by latticework fencing full of trellised roses. She'd drawn a beautiful English garden with a set of water fountains and a bench where a box of postcards sat.

She'd always wondered about that box of postcards. In every image her mom had drawn, the same box of postcards could be found, whether on a table outside a little café in Paris or on the steps of the Colosseum where a horse-drawn carriage waited for its next riders.

She used to ask her dad about it, the significance of postcards, but all he would say was that they were people's stories written down, just like the ones in her mom's study.

For the longest time, Abby thought the idea of having your life story written on one tiny postcard was sad. There should be more to life than what you could write down in that little space, right? As she grew older, she thought that maybe that's what the box was for . . . that all those postcards in that box were the stories of your life—written down one moment at a time.

It made sense. She wished her mom had a box full of moments that she could read through. All her life, all she'd wanted was to know her mother better. She had her journals and letters but there had to be more . . . right?

NINE

MILLIE

A dance troop of jitterbugs was holding dress rehearsals in Millie's stomach, and it wasn't a pleasant sensation.

Between Josh's terse text messages and Abby's barrage of messages with concerns about where they were staying and what they would or could or should do during their trip, Millie was close to canceling the whole thing.

Call it last minute regrets or bad memories or . . . hell, she was an old woman. What was she thinking taking her twenty-year-old granddaughter to Europe?

Thank God for David. After putting up with her foolishness for more than three hours this morning, he'd finally made a pot of tea and told her to stop being silly.

Silly. He actually used that word. He'd told her a few other things as well, like that she should pull up her big-girl panties, maybe drinking that hot toddy before bed wasn't a smart idea, and she might want to consider not letting the past dictate her present.

Truth be told, it was the big-girl panties part that hurt the most.

Like Josh, the last time she'd been to Europe had been with Claire. She'd taken her to Europe to help Claire heal the wound of giving her child up for adoption, in the misguided hope the change of scenery would make all the difference in the world.

She'd been wrong. So very, very wrong.

Motherhood was the hardest job on the planet. She'd made so many mistakes—too many, she knew—but remaining silent while she watched her husband force Claire to give her child up for adoption . . . that was one she would forever regret.

After the adoption, Millie took Claire to Great Britain, where they toured the island, staying in old and drafty castles in Scotland, stopping in Bath, and visiting other cities in England before coming back home. The trip hadn't helped, not in the way she'd foolishly hoped it would. The emptiness in her daughter's gaze . . . it took years for that expression to stop haunting her dreams.

She wasn't sure she could handle going back to London. Germany and Belgium—that was fine. But London. She'd sworn never to go back to that city, and she couldn't help but fear she was making a grave error.

It was David who convinced her that two days in the city wouldn't hurt. In fact, going to Blossom Lane, to the bed-and-breakfast where her daughter had stayed, might even help heal those deep wounds.

She hoped he was right.

As Millie sat across from her granddaughter, she could see that Abby was agitated, the poor soul.

"How long have you been stressing over this?" Millie asked Abby.

Through the two cups of mint tea Millie had been sipping, Abby had asked question after question about the trip. It was exhausting. She'd had an inkling that Abby was a bit of a control freak, but until now she hadn't realized the extent.

And she'd thought Claire had been bad.

"I was fine until I opened my laptop and googled the bed-and-breakfast place in London." Abby nibbled on her lip.

"I've got it covered, Abby. Can you trust me on this?"

"I know, but,"—Abby's leg bounced fitfully until she finally pulled it tight to her chest, resting the heel on the seat of her chair—"the bed-and-breakfast in London that my parents stayed in is now closed."

Millie glanced over at Sam, who was leaning against the wall.

"I've got it covered, Abby," Millie repeated.

"But—" Abby swallowed audibly.

"Abigail Turner." Millie's sharp tone made Abby sit up straight. "Give me a little bit of credit, please and thank you." She gave a pointed look to Abby's finger, which was hopping at the edge of the table like a pogo-stick jumper.

Tap tap tap tap tap tap tap—a hollow hammering sound against the wood.

Abby pulled her finger back into a tight fist and blushed.

"I'm sorry, I just . . ." It was clear Abby couldn't quite get the words out.

"Yes, Blossom Lane is now closed and is only a private residence," Millie confirmed, "but it's still owned by the same family. I received a reply from my e-mail this morning, and we've been invited for tea."

Abby's shoulders sagged with obvious relief.

"Well, thank goodness for that!" Sam said. "See, Abby. I told you getting all worked up wasn't going to do any good." Sam sipped her coffee. "You need to relax, girl."

"I'm relaxed." The scowl on Abby's face made Millie snort. Abby's right hand was still clenched while her other gripped her coffee cup a little too tightly. She jumped up from her chair. "Millie—more hot water for your tea?"

With a glance at her half-full mug, Millie nodded.

"Are you wanting to stay in London, sweets, or are you anxious to get the German leg of the trip started?" Millie reached for her notebook. A large part of her couldn't help wishing Abby would say she'd like to skip London completely, but she'd settle for keeping it to a day. Maybe two.

On her way to the house, she'd called her husband's niece, Justyna, to see where she was with their various travel options. She wanted Abby's input, but some arrangements couldn't be made last minute, although, technically this whole trip was last minute.

Not if she wanted to keep her own jitters in check. She wasn't as young as she used to be. Her last big trip had been more years ago than she wanted to remember. The quick honeymoon cruise to the Caribbean with David didn't count—she'd felt so loved, there'd been no room for anything else.

Abby turned the question around. "Is there anything in London you'd like to see, Millie? Do you think we could stay at the bed-and-breakfast, even though—"

"Abby, it's closed," Sam reminded her.

"We're going for tea," Millie repeated. "And please do not answer my questions with another question." Millie tapped her pen. David told her to spend an afternoon at Harrods—have a cuppa in their tearoom, buy chocolates from their candy store, and stroll through the fashion section, gasping at the ridiculous prices for scarfs; she could even buy herself one if it was on sale.

"I imagine London and Paris would be lovely in the spring. Maybe we could plan a return trip?" There was a sparkle in her granddaughter's gaze, a sparkle full of life, of promise, and of happiness. It was so good to see Abby like this—so vivacious with energy.

"Backpacking through Europe would be kind of fun," Sam mused, as she stood off to the side.

The speed of Abby's head whipping around toward Sam gave Millie a chuckle.

"Would you do that with me, Sam?" Abby said dreamily, as if she couldn't quite believe what she was hearing.

"As long as we can stay in nice hotels and Specks could come, I'm in." She set her mug down and held her arms out.

"Shut up!" Abby rushed to enfold Sam in the hug she'd been waiting for. "You're not freakin' kidding me, right? You won't back out? You're serious? Like really serious? Cause you can't just throw that out there and then take it back." Abby leaned out, holding Sam at arm's length. "There are no take backs."

Sam gave quite the dramatic sigh, then looked over at Millie and winked.

"This might be easier on your father than our other idea. We can do London, Paris, Venice, and Rome, similar to what your parents did. That way you don't need to feel like you have to see it all in one trip."

Abby squealed. "I love you! You know that, right?"

Listening to the girls eased something inside of Millie she didn't realize had been at all tense.

"Sounds like the perfect strategy, girls. But, how about we plan one trip at a time?" With a glance at her watch, Millie pointed toward Abby's empty chair. "Sit, girl. I don't have all day."

Abby sat, but her body wouldn't hold still. She buzzed with an energy Millie couldn't get enough of.

"Okay, London. Let's just do a day or two there. Long enough for afternoon tea and a beer with fish and chips in an old pub before we head to"—Millie caught Abby peering into her notebook—"Belgium."

"Belgium." The word slipped from Abby's mouth like a whispered prayer. "Bruges? Brussels?"

"Both," said Millie.

"By train or . . . ?"

Millie nodded. "Well, we have two options, really. We can make it our first Christmas market stop, or we can make it our last."

"Last." Abby didn't even hesitate.

"Are you sure?" Millie was curious now. "It really doesn't matter to me either way."

"Last. I'm sure. In one of the letters Mom wrote to me, she said that the day she and dad spent in Bruges included one of the best moments of her year."

Millie remembered that. Claire believed in taking those minuscule moments and holding them close.

"Let's do this then: We'll head to Brussels the last few days of our trip. We'll take a day trip to Bruges, since they apparently have quite the quaint Christmas market and"—she peeked at her notes—"a lot of chocolate shops."

"Fifty, to be exact," Sam said.

Millie looked at her. "Fifty? Really?"

"According to the book Claire made for Abby. She wrote something in there about fifty chocolate shops, didn't she?"

Abby nodded. "Yep. Remember, Millie? The little girl in the book bought one chocolate at each shop. I don't think I could do that, though."

Sam chortled. "I dare you *not* to try. In fact, I double-dog dare you to not eat at least one piece of chocolate at every shop you see."

"Double-dog dare—"

Millie heard the challenge in Abby's voice and saw the laughter on her face. "Now wait a minute." Millie held up her hand. "I happen to like chocolate. And if I remember correctly, this was something your father actually accomplished when they were there. If he can do it, there's no reason why we can't." They might end up with a bellyache, but it would be worth it. Belgian chocolate was some of the best in the world, or so she'd been told. She rather liked the idea of finding out for herself.

"Back to the itinerary, girls." If she didn't rein things in, this trip would never get sorted out. "We'll enjoy Bruges for the day and then go back to Belgium for the night. Their market is supposed to be spectacular. Their square is lit up with dancing lights timed in perfect unison with classical music. After a little bit of shopping, we'll sit and people watch."

Millie saw the look of hesitation on Abby's face.

"Spit it out," Millie said. She couldn't stand people not speaking their minds.

"Do you . . ." Abby stared down into her coffee mug and gnawed delicately on her lip. "Do you think maybe Dad would join us? Just for the last days of our trip? Maybe bring David? We could make it a real Christmas trip. Maybe even stay on closer to Christmas? Wouldn't that be awesome—to spend Christmas Day there? Think of how happy Mom would be, how much she would have loved that." She swallowed hard, as if the words had been forced out and they hurt along the way.

"I think . . ." Now it was Millie who paused to swallow. Her voice had coiled tight like a rough rope dried up, and her words scraped out. "Your mom would have done exactly that. Well, maybe she'd come home Christmas Eve," she said, backtracking. "Your mom really didn't like spending Christmas Day anywhere but here, in the heart of her circle of family and friends." Millie stared up at the ceiling. "She swore that waking up surrounded by the ones that truly made the moments of life worthwhile was the best present of all." Millie shook her head and blinked rapidly. She would not tear up, would not cry, would not let herself become emotional.

She was planning a trip, damn it, not meandering down memory lane.

"We'll do that then," Abby said softly, her voice like a cashmere scarf settling over a cold neck. Comforting. Soothing. Full of heart and warmth. "Dad has to come. He just has to."

"Abby . . ." There was a note of caution mixed with love in Sam's voice, a note that Millie recognized and felt the truth of.

She wasn't sure Josh could come. It wasn't that he wouldn't, or didn't want to, but more that he would be emotionally unable to handle the trip.

She'd never known a man more in love with a woman, and as much as she wanted him to find happiness, she also felt keenly the honor of knowing her daughter had been loved so fiercely.

Every woman should know that type of love.

Every woman deserved that type of love.

Every woman needed that type of love.

It was a once-in-a-lifetime type of love, and no one could fault Josh for it.

"I'll ask him." Abby set her jaw. Millie knew that look all too well. Her granddaughter was determined, and nothing would stop her.

"Just don't push too hard, love. And don't be upset if he says no," Millie warned.

"He'll come. He has to."

"Oh, Abby." The disappointment in Sam's voice rang out clearly, like an old-fashioned dinner bell calling farm folks in for dinner. There was no mistaking how Sam felt about Abby's resolve. "Just because you wish it, doesn't mean it's going to happen. Your father has done so much for you—so much. But *this,* this might be asking too much."

Millie looked over at Sam, who was like a member of the family, and felt so much love for the woman she'd become. She prayed Abby would listen to her and would hear, *really* hear, what Sam said and take it to heart.

"All I can do is ask. There's no harm in that. If Dad says no, then he says no. But I won't know until I ask him and hear him say it to me himself. It's been twenty years. He has to grow out of . . . of whatever it is that stops him from living life sometime." Abby held her mug of coffee close to her face, as if hiding from the harshness of her own words.

"He is living life. His life. The way he wants to," Sam rebutted. "That life, it's centered on you, and you know it. Just because you now have the freedom to start living the life you feel has always been out of reach doesn't mean he has to do that too." Irritation crept into Sam's voice, and Millie could see from the way Abby stiffened that if she didn't step in, things could go sour fast.

"Ask him, honey. For sure. But if he says no, accept that, okay?" Millie leaned back and forced a smile onto her face. "So, back to our trip. After London, I thought we'd just head straight to Germany. Specifically, Munich. Your mother and I had lists and lists of towns to visit that are all basically day trips from Munich. Are you okay with that?"

Abby nodded.

"Good. Justyna is going to work on creating an itinerary and hiring a tour guide for us. At my age, adventurousness only goes so far . . . I'd rather not have to deal with train schedules, hotels, transportation, or even finding places to eat every day."

Abby leaned forward. "But Millie, where's that travel spirit of yours? What happened to just getting lost and finding the moments to enjoy?"

She was happy to see Abby's contentious look from earlier had disappeared. "Honey"—Millie gathered up her notebook and tucked it back into her bag—"I deserve a little pampering, don't you think? We'll be adventurous. We'll travel and see all the things we have on our list and find all the others we didn't know about. And we'll get lost—as long as our guide knows how to find us."

Abby played with her coffee mug, twirling it in circles on the table, creating water stains as she did so.

"What's on your mind?" Millie asked.

Abby shook her head. "Nothing. Something. Everything." She glanced up, a hint of a smile gracing her lips. "This is going to be amazing, isn't it?"

Millie leaned forward and lightly touched her granddaughter's hand. "*Amazing* isn't even the word for it. I think it'll be *life changing, dream fulfilling, moment creating*. All three combined in one. This has been a dream of mine for too many years to count."

"Mom would be so happy, wouldn't she?" Abby's voice quavered.

The words Millie wanted to say wouldn't come out, which Sam must have noticed.

Sam said, "Your mom is happy, honey. She's probably up there, in heaven, chatting everyone's ear off about how much you're going to love this trip. She'll be there with you, every step of the way. You'll feel her presence too—I have no doubt about that." Sam stood next to Abby, her hand resting on her shoulder.

"Do you feel her, Sam? My mom? Do you feel her in your life?"

There was a moment of stillness in the kitchen, a peaceful silence that settled among the three of them.

"All the time, love. All the time."

TEN

CLAIRE

To be read before your first real vacation.

Right now, your passport is empty, but if you're anything like me, as you grow up, you'll quickly fill up all those pages with stamps from different countries around the world.

Where is your first trip? Who are you going with? Are you alone or with your father or grandmother?

Have you read my travel journal yet? If not, this is a great time to ask your grandmother about it. She has a special trip in store for you—I can't wait till you go!

If I know your father, he's reluctant to take you any place that isn't surrounded by trees, water, and wildlife.

If I know my mother, she's the one taking you on this trip.

Where will you go, Abby?

I hope you take after me. Your father calls me a travelholic. I won't deny it—it's something I've always wanted to do.

My favorite place to travel is Europe. I hope that one day you can see Italy. Rome is rich with history, the

Amalfi coast is breathtaking, and the food—you can't get enough of it. Pasta, pizza, fresh fruit, and the lemons . . . oh, the lemons. Make sure you go to Positano and see Miima and Rocco Almonti. Your father and I stayed at their lovely bed-and-breakfast—Casa delle Memorie— and you would love it. Miima also makes the best espresso.

I have some advice for when you go on your first real trip. When I say real, *I mean when you're an adult, when you've helped to plan either a portion or all of the trip, when it's more than just Disneyland and roller coaster rides.*

Carry your camera. If you're not comfortable yet with photography, take some courses.

Bring a journal and write about your day, every day.

Send yourself postcards from the places you've been. Tell yourself the best stories of the day.

Look for the moments that can change your life. They will always be there.

Talk to the locals. Listen to them, ask them questions, hear their stories.

Eat the local food. Try their drinks. Enjoy their customs.

Try something new every day. Go out of your comfort zone.

Explore. Go off the beaten path.

I hope you enjoy it. I hope it becomes a passion you indulge in again and again and again.

I wish I were there with you.

xoxo,

Mom

ELEVEN

ABBY

Hey Dad,

London is amazing, and I'm writing like I promised! I'll send a postcard a day. We'll see if you get them before I get home or not.

The hotel is more than I'd expected. Did you know they have butlers here? The only downside to this trip is that Millie snores. Did you know that? Of course you didn't know . . . poor David. I should have taken the hint when he handed me earplugs, I guess.

Today we're playing tourists. Tomorrow we are to be "civilized Canadians," or so Millie says. Yes, Dad, I rolled my eyes at her. You would too. You'd think we were about to have tea with the queen. I should add that to my list . . . I wonder if it was something Mom had added to hers once?

Our tea with the family you stayed with is making me nervous, and I'm not really certain why. I'm sure it'll be fine. It will be, right?

I feel fine. No cold. No sneezing. No runny nose. I know you're worried. I promise I'm feeling absolutely fabulous.

I love you, Dad.

Love, your Gabby Abby (who will probably be tongue-tied today)

PS. I wish you were here.

TWELVE

ABBY

Abby's Journey: A Personal Blog

Trip of a Lifetime: Day Two

Yesterday was . . . amazing. It's not possible to spend the day at Harrods and not feel like a princess—especially if you dress up for it. If you are ever in London, take my word for it: put on your prettiest dress, wear your most comfortable flats, and head to Harrods for a cup of tea. While you're there, wander through the clothing departments and try on a few items here and there. Don't skip the tea and chocolate departments downstairs, and be prepared to ship home a full box of all the various teas, teacups, teapots, and boxes of chocolates you buy. It's addictive, and your credit card (or in this case, Dad's credit card) might not thank you for it, but when you return home and feel nostalgia about all your adventures, sipping the tea you bought in the teacup you just couldn't pass up . . . you'll be transported back to here.

Or, so I'm told. Anyway, that's the line I was fed by the person selling me that teacup. And I bought it hook, line, and sinker.

Another thing—it's not possible to spend only two days in London. Yesterday was a whirlwind. Between tea at Harrods and then taking the Hop-On, Hop-Off bus tour and quickly seeing the sights before we both collapsed from exhaustion, I couldn't wait to crawl into bed. Guess coming back to London will be another thing on my list of places to visit . . . I want to really experience the places I visit, not just whiz through them and take photos to say I was here.

Now, off to write some promised postcards.

PS. We can scratch "fish and chips with mushy peas" off the list of things to try. Same with bangers and mash. I'm a huge fan! Hey, Mr. Mike: you should serve this in the pub!

Abby tucked her closed laptop into her bag and wiped her eyes, hoping Millie wouldn't catch her crying.

She was just tired. Her body felt like it could sleep for another eight hours, which wasn't good. She was exhausted from the long travel day—she hadn't slept on the flight at all—and then adjusting to having earplugs in her ears to drown out Millie's snoring didn't help either.

There was no way she was homesick after being here a little more than twenty-four hours.

It surprised her how hard it'd been to leave her dad at the airport. She could still feel the weight of his arms as he hugged her close, and she knew it had been hard for him to let her go.

He'd made her promise to text him daily, to come home the moment she felt a cold coming on, and to not exhaust herself, knowing her body was most susceptible when she was tired.

She'd text him, sure. But she also wanted to send him postcards. Every day.

She'd asked him to join them, to fly in and meet them toward the end of their trip, but he'd said no. Perhaps by sending him the postcards, sharing her adventures with him, he'd be more willing to come on the next trip with her.

Because there would be more trips. Of that, she had no doubt.

Just as she knew she wouldn't get sick again—not now at least.

"Ready?" Millie stepped out of the bathroom, and Abby's mouth fell open.

"What . . . what are you . . . *who* are you?"

Millie stood there looking so regal, and so non-Millie-ish.

Millie's style consisted of yoga pants, comfy shoes, and bright, bold, and bodacious tops. Not . . . this.

This was a solid black dress with the gorgeous pink scarf that she bought at Harrods yesterday. Abby couldn't believe the price for a simple scrap of fabric, or the price of most anything in that store, and yet, Millie handed over her credit card like a giddy schoolgirl. She giggled. She actually giggled as she held the scarf in her hands, fingers caressing the fabric.

This was black flats and nylons—nylons for Pete's sake.

This was a small hat resting atop of her hair—hair that wasn't flya-way or curly or anything that was normally Millie-ish. Her hair was smooth and straight and . . .

"*Wow.*"

"Wow? Is that a good *wow* or a bad *wow*?" Millie bit her lip while her fingers clenched and unclenched.

"That's a what-happened-to-my-quirky-grandmother *wow*. A who-the-hell-are-you *wow*. That was a—"

Millie giggled, the sound similar to a four-year-old girl in a tickle war with her father.

"You do realize you're giggling, right?" Abby shook her head, still attempting to digest what she was seeing.

"You would too if you could see the look on your face. Good to know I've still got it."

"Should I change?" With a glance at her jeans, black ankle boots, and soft, black merino wool winter jacket, Abby saw that she was com-pletely underdressed. She thought about the clothes she'd brought, and nothing—and she meant *nothing*—was suitable.

"Yes, Abby, you need to change. Good thing I bought you a dress, isn't it?" Millie winked as she smoothed the fabric of her dress down over her hips.

"A dress? Where? Wait—you bought me a dress? Why? Please tell me I don't have to wear a hat and scarf and . . ." Abby glanced around the room, looking around for this dress Millie apparently bought.

"In the bathroom, love. Go look. No hat, but there is something extra I have for you when you're dressed. And of course you'll wear a scarf. It's winter, in case you haven't noticed." Millie stepped further into the room. "Stop staring, Abby," Millie said with a hint of laughter in her voice.

"I need to take a photo." Abby reached for her phone. "Dad will never believe it." She waited for Millie to pose before snapping a shot and texting her father.

"What are you saying?" Millie tried to read her message.

Abby held it up.

Dad, proof Millie can be taken out!

"Oh, you did not." Millie took the phone from her hands and then prodded her toward the bathroom. "Go on. Your turn."

Abby stepped into the bathroom and whistled when she saw the dress hanging behind the door. It was similar to Millie's except in a soft gray. She held it up to her body and noticed the hem ended at her knees. On the floor were a pair of black flats, and a package of black tights rested on the counter. The dress itself looked a little plain, but the fabric was so soft, and she had a feeling it would be quite flattering on her slender frame.

"Well, look at you." Millie put her hand over her heart and sighed. "I knew you were a dress girl."

"I'm so not a dress girl, Millie. You know that."

"Well, you could be a dress girl. You've just never found out. You don't want to go out all the time wearing jeans or yoga pants, do you? A woman needs to have something in her wardrobe that makes her feel . . . girly."

Millie held up the phone in her hand and snapped a photo. Before Abby could grab the phone from her, Millie texted furiously, an enigmatic smile on her face.

"What did you say?" Abby checked the message and groaned.

I'm not the only one who can be taken out. Doesn't our girl look beautiful? She'll have boys beating a path to her door, but don't worry, I'll only encourage the nicest ones.

"'Hello' said the match to the candlewick," Abby muttered as she reread the text message. She didn't even want to think about her father's reply. He'll probably demand that she return home right away.

"He needs a few challenges if he wants to learn to adjust better," Millie teased, her face all aglow, as Abby's cheeks reddened.

"Weren't you the one agreeing with Sam—that he doesn't need to be pushed too hard?" Abby glanced at the time, wanting, needing to change the subject. "Shouldn't we be going?"

She'd never had a serious boyfriend, never even really had a crush on a boy. Sure, she knew some. They were either from her online classes or from her stays in the hospital. But that connection, the kind that her parents had, was never there.

"Our taxi is probably already waiting. I called the concierge to arrange for one while you were changing." Millie grabbed her coat and purse before pausing. "One last thing, though. I've been waiting forever to give you this." She reached into her purse and pulled out a small jewelry box.

"This was your mother's." Millie's voice softened as Abby opened the lid. "She asked me to wait to give it to you, until we could take a trip together." Millie's lips twitched. "I think she meant for you to get it before now, but—"

"It's . . ." Abby blinked, once, twice. The necklace was . . . not quite *beautiful,* but more . . . She searched her mind for the word she wanted but couldn't find it.

"Sweet? Endearing? Precious? Special?" Millie suggested, her lips quirking in a knowing smile.

"Awesome and perfect," Abby said instead.

The necklace was a gold-plated engraved rectangle attached to the chain by two small globes that looked like the world on either side of the bar. The word? *Wanderlust.*

"She always meant for me to travel, didn't she?" Abby swallowed past the rock lodged tight in her throat.

"She wanted to share the world with you."

Abby blinked away the tears pooling in her eyes and lifted her hair so Millie could help her with the necklace. She fingered the gold bar, tracing the word, memorizing it.

"Did she wear this?"

Millie smoothed her hair down, curling it over her shoulders before gently touching the necklace.

Abby wasn't the only one struggling not to cry.

"I bought it for her on our first trip. She was younger than you, and . . ." Millie paused, her brow wrinkling before she gave her head a small shake.

"And . . . ?" Abby prodded.

"And nothing. I found this in a shop here, actually. The hotel we'd stayed in had a lovely little gift shop, and I noticed her looking at it. I bought it as a surprise, and she wore it . . . for a long time afterwards." Millie took a deep breath and pushed her shoulders back. "Enough of that—we need to run. You look beautiful, and you're about to experience your first English tea. Are you ready?"

Abby had so many questions she wanted to ask. Like what had Millie been about to say? Why wouldn't she ever really talk about that trip? This wasn't the first time she'd mentioned it, nor was it the first time she'd changed the subject shortly after bringing it up. Her mother only briefly touched on that first trip to England in her letters, which left Abby wondering whether something had happened.

Over the years, she'd considered different possibilities, trying to piece the puzzle together. Maybe she'd fallen in love with a young Brit who broke her heart or maybe she'd left someone back at home who ended up cheating on her, thus breaking her heart when she returned. In every scenario, her mother always had a broken heart. It was the one emotion Abby took away from the brief mention.

Instead of asking the questions that were on the tip of her tongue, she reached for her grandmother's hand and squeezed.

"I'm ready for a new adventure." She gave Millie a kiss on the cheek and then held the necklace between her fingers. "Thank you . . . for this. It means so much to me." She couldn't put into words how much having her mother's necklace meant to her.

Growing up, she'd received little things, here and there, from her mother. Things her father thought she was ready to have—her mother's pencil set when she'd signed up for watercolor lessons held at the hospital; small knickknacks collected during their travels, like a paper holder in the shape of the Eiffel Tower; or a jar of seashells when Abby asked to go on a beach vacation.

There was a light blush on Millie's cheek. "You remind me so much of her. Sometimes you steal my breath away. You've turned into a beautiful young girl, Abigail Turner, just like your mother knew you would." She patted Abby's hand before she could say anything in reply, leading the way out of their hotel room and on to their next adventure.

THIRTEEN

ABBY

During the drive through the city, while bracing herself for the turns, Abby stared out the window, taking in all the sights. As the cab driver swerved again, Millie grabbed hold of Abby's hand, squeezing tight. Millie's face was as white as a poached egg, her eyes barely open while the fingers of her other hand worried the straps of her purse. But the hint of a smile—while they sat together in the backseat swaying side to side, their driver navigating avenues, side streets, and perhaps even the odd cobblestone walkway—told Abby all she needed to know.

They pulled up to a quaint little cottage across from a park.

Abby smothered her laughter as Millie exited the cab, her hands shaking as she paid the driver.

"Maybe we'll walk back," Millie said under her breath once Abby had closed the cab door and was wrapping her arm around her grandmother's waist.

"Oh, come on, now. That was quite fun," Abby teased.

It hadn't been just fun, it had been exhilarating and memory making and . . . *wild*. The way people drive in London is pure craziness. It's like drivers don't even see the road lines. And the streets—they were definitely not created for anything but horse-drawn carriages.

A small smile teased at the corner of Millie's lips as she adjusted her scarf.

"Say it . . . ," Abby prompted.

"Okay." Millie gave in. "It was fun." They'd arrived at the walkway to the house, and she peeked at her watch and then turned to look at the park. "We've got a few minutes. Do you want to take a walk?"

Abby glanced down at the flats they wore. Their shoes were designed for walks through stores and bakeries and for enjoying tea at the Ritz, not for walking along English garden paths in the middle of December. She was thankful there was no snow on the ground.

"Hello." A sweet voice called out from behind them. Both Millie and Abby pivoted, to see a small girl at the front door. "Mum said you looked lost. Are you our guests for tea?"

"I think so." Abby made her way to the door and held out her hand to the little girl who waited for them. By her bright smile, ruddy cheeks, and adorable swaying pigtails, Abby figured her to be about six years or so.

"I'm Abby Turner, and this is my grandmother Millie." She couldn't help but smile as she noticed the little girl attempt to conceal the chocolate on her hands, wiping them on the back of her pants.

"I'm Katherine Elizabeth," she said, her chin pointed outward before she thrust out her chocolate-streaked hand.

"Katy, love, don't be standing there with the door open. We're not heating the outdoors, remember?" Katy's mother appeared in the background, wiping her hands on her apron before resting them on her daughter's shoulders.

"Welcome. You must be Mrs. Jeffries and Ms. Turner. Katy here saw you pull up in the cab. Come in, please." She stepped to the side, leading Katy along with her.

"This is Penny, my mum." Katy's wide smile beamed brightly and even somewhat cheekily, while Penny, her mother, shook her head.

"I'll introduce myself, little duck, thank you very much." Penny reached for her daughter's pigtail and tugged, amusement shining through her smile while Katy looked up and gave an impish grin.

"Charlie is out back. Katy, why don't you go get your da, *hmm*?"

Little Katy skipped down the hall and out of sight, humming a Christmas song that sounded like a cross between "Rudolph, the Red-Nosed Reindeer" and "Winter Wonderland."

"She must keep you on your toes." Millie shrugged out of her coat and handed it to Penny, who stood waiting, hanger in hand.

"Oh, that she does. She's a lot like her father in that sense. She didn't smother you in chocolate, did she?" Penny glanced at Abby's hands. "She was icing the cupcakes as you arrived."

"No"—Abby held out her hands—"chocolate-free."

Abby trailed after Millie as they made their way through the English home. She wondered how much it had remained the same from the time when her parents had been here. Did that antique table sit in that same spot by the wall, with the washbasin full of flowers? Were the photos on the walls different? What had her mom thought the moment she walked in?

She paused before entering what she assumed was the sitting room. Soft light from the windows bathed the room, and at once, Abby felt at home. The walls were lined with shelves full of books and odd curios. In the corner was a little reading area complete with comfy chairs and a short table stacked with more books. To one side was a larger table, and on it a tray with teacups, a teapot, and two cake platters piled with scones, tiny sandwiches, and chocolate-frosted cupcakes.

There was an older woman sitting in one of the chairs, an afghan covering her legs. She held a cup in her hands as if using the cup to warm herself, and her shoulders were hunched, giving her a frail appearance.

"Please, sit while I go check on Charlie and see what's keeping him. The tea should be ready soon. It's just now steeping." Penny quickly left before either Abby or Millie could say a word.

While Millie sat, Abby walked around the room, her fingers trailing across the spines of the books filling the shelves. There were so many, all hardcovers, and for a moment as she closed her eyes, Abby imagined she was Belle, lost in her own wonderland.

Abby paid no attention to Millie, who sat across from the older woman, their voices a soft cadence in the room. Instead, she read through the titles, wishing she could pull them out and really peruse them. Was this how her mother had felt, in this room all those years ago? She'd written about the bright room full of books, of curling up in one of the chairs and reading to her heart's content. Which chair had she sat in? Which book would she have read?

"Abby, come join us," Millie called out to her, tearing her from her thoughts. "There is someone who would love to meet you."

Abby turned to find the older woman's gaze resting on her, a wisp of a smile on her face.

"You look just like her," she said as Abby stepped closer. "Your mother was so beautiful. Her heart was heavy and her smile sad, but there was a joy inside of her that I can never forget."

Abby looked toward Millie who had tears in her eyes.

"I'm Lolly, dear. Your sweet parents stayed with us when we had our home open for guests," Lolly explained.

Abby reached out for the woman's hands, taking the tea from her grasp and setting it to the side. She sat down on the ottoman on the right and looked deep into Lolly's gaze.

"My mother wrote me stories about you, about your talks and the cups of tea you would share." Abby couldn't believe she was actually talking with Lolly. She must have been at least seventy years old.

This was too good to be true.

"We had a lot of people come through our doors, and it wasn't often that a real friendship developed, but your mother was one I will never forget. Your parents stayed here for a few weeks, but when they left, it felt like I was losing someone close." Lolly closed her

eyes. "She wrote me a few times, before she passed"—she opened
her eyes, and it was as if Abby could see into her soul, they were so
clear and bright—"before you were born. I heard from your father
as well, now and then. He would send me photos of you when you
were younger." Lolly leaned forward, cupping Abby's cheeks between
her cold hands. "You have her eyes. So beautiful. Just like your
grandmother's too."

"Abby reminds me a lot of Claire. She's almost her spitting image."
Millie cleared her throat.

"Nanny, you're making them cry." Little Katy's voice broke in, and
Lolly released her hold on Abby's face and leaned back. She glanced at
Millie, who was wiping the corners of her eyes, then set her eyes on the
little girl, who entered the room carrying a box.

"We old women have the tendency to do that, chicken." Lolly
leaned back in her chair, hand outstretched.

Abby handed her back her barely warm cup of tea.

"Mum says it's time for tea, and Da is washing his hands. I get to
hand out the plates." With the air of someone who takes her responsi-
bilities seriously, Katy placed the box down at her grandmother's feet
before heading to the table with the sandwiches and desserts.

Abby watched as she filled plates with a triangle-sliced sandwich,
a small cookie, and a mini cupcake slathered with chocolate icing.
She then brought the plate over to Lolly, setting it on the small table
beside her.

"Thank you for joining us for afternoon tea." Penny stepped into
the room, a warm smile on her face as she took in the scene. "I see
Katy's started to hand out the little treats. How do you take your tea?
Mrs. Jeffries?"

"Millie, please. And I like it black, thank you." Millie crossed her
ankles and held her hands primly in her lap.

"Sorry for my tardiness."

The man who entered the room was probably in his mid-thirties, and he wore a sweater, cream colored with large brown buttons, that was a little reminiscent of Mr. Rogers.

"That's my son, Charlie. Your mother met him, Abby." Lolly's weathered eyes watered at the mention.

"I was only a young lad, but I will never forget the famous authors who came to stay in our home. Katy likes to read those stories before bed, don't you, love?"

"Jack is awesome!" Katy piped up as she handed out another plate full of goodies. Except, this time there were two sandwiches, two cookies, and two cupcakes on Millie's plate.

"Jack is awesome," Abby agreed.

"It's too bad your father stopped writing stories about the boy." Charlie took the tea tray from Penny and brought it over to them.

"Josh took some time off from writing once Abby was born," Millie said as if that explained the chaos and grief of those early years.

"Of course he did. That's what parents do—focus on their children when they're young. Is he still writing?" Lolly asked as she held out her cup to be refilled.

Abby nodded.

Katy gasped and almost dropped the plate she held. "You mean there's more Jack stories?" Her face lit up, and her body bounced with energy.

"Oh, sorry, Katy. No more Jack books. He's writing grown-up things now." Abby hated to disappoint the little girl. Maybe she could convince her dad to write a quick little story using one of mom's old drawings, one that hadn't been used in their previous books, and send it to Katy as a gift?

"What's your favorite one? I have one. Want to see it? It's in my room. I know it all by heart, and your mom even signed it. I'll go get it if you want to see it." Katy paused for a breath before turning to her mom. "Is that okay?"

"I think that will be fine. Take your time, love." Penny winked at her daughter. "Let the adults talk for a little bit, okay?"

With Katy gone, the silence in the room snuck up on everyone, creating awkward pauses as they sipped their tea. Charlie gamely fielded Abby's questions about tea—about the difference between high tea and afternoon tea, and whether the queen really served her dogs tea in the afternoon, or if that was just a silly thing her parents had made up for Jack's story set in London.

Both Charlie and Penny laughed at her last question and then pointed to one of the cookies on the tray.

Abby couldn't believe she'd missed the dog-biscuit-shaped treat.

"Every morning, or so we've been told, the queen likes to have her morning tea with her corgis at her feet. They get their own biscuits and water. Katy picked out the dog-biscuit cookie cutter last year on a tour of Kensington Palace once Charlie pointed out the connection to Jack." Penny smiled at her husband.

"She really likes the Jack books then? Even though they're quite old?" Millie leaned forward and balanced her teacup on her knee.

"They were the first books Charlie would read to her at bedtime," Lolly broke in. "Having your parents here was really quite the occasion. Charlie was just a boy and had his own Jack copy your parents signed. They were quite possibly our most famous guests."

"I don't think that really mattered to my parents," Abby said softly.

Lolly looked at her for a moment before nodding her head. "No, you're right. That didn't seem to matter at all. In fact, the more we tried to draw information out of them, the more they would ask questions of us. I had a lot of stories to tell, so I didn't mind, not really." Lolly glanced down at the box at her feet. "You're here for your mother's story though, aren't you?"

Abby stared at the box. It looked like a shoe box, but made out of wood. There was no lid, and for some reason, it looked familiar to Abby.

It was the same box full of postcards her mother had drawn in the book she'd made for her.

"You're probably wondering about this box." Lolly blinked a few times and ran her finger along the rim of her cup.

"My mom drew some pictures that contained a box really similar to yours," Abby said. She glanced at Millie, to see if she recognized it. Millie nodded back.

"I'm not surprised." Lolly smiled. "When my parents opened up the bed-and-breakfast, they started a tradition, one that I carried on and told your mom about. My father built this box, and we kept it on the bookshelves here in this room. Your mother wrote a few notes and letters while she was here. I remember her being sad a lot, almost as if she were grieving." She shook her head, as if remembering something she didn't want to. "I never asked. We had so many people come to the cottage who needed a rest of some sort, and I figured your parents were the same. It's why," she said, pointing to the box, "I showed her these. This box is full of postcards from those who needed to leave a piece of their heart behind. Your mother was one of them."

"She was sad?" Abby looked to her grandmother, who sat holding the cup of tea in her hands, shoulders stiff. But Millie kept her gaze focused on the box at Lolly's side.

"Some she mailed off," Lolly said. "One she left in this box, and then there's the one," she said, turning toward her son, "you found one in their room after they left, didn't you Charlie?"

Charlie nodded. "It's still there, Mum. Along with her small gift. Abby, I can take you to see it after you've finished your tea."

Abby had to suppress the urge to tell him to take her there now. She gulped some of her tea and sputtered as the hot liquid burned down her throat.

"You kept it there after all these years?" Abby asked.

Charlie smiled. "It's our claim to fame and holds a lot of meaning for us, which was more important. We figured your mother left it there for a purpose, and so there it remained."

"Can I . . . can we . . . see the note in the box?" Millie asked.

Charlie handed the box to his mother, who slowly opened it and went through it, a soft smile gracing her face as she leafed through the cards.

"There are so many stories in here. Claire loved to go through it while sitting in this room, drinking her tea," Lolly said to Millie as she pulled out a postcard. "This one—this one is meant for you, I believe. The other would be for her daughter."

"The child of her heart," Penny said softly.

There was a tug at Abby's heart at the words. She'd read them so often, it was a phrase her mother had repeated in various journal entries.

Lolly handed the card to Millie, who hesitated briefly before taking it. Millie's eyes skittered toward Abby for a brief moment.

The room was silent while Millie read her postcard, eyes glistening as she mouthed the words before holding the postcard tight to her chest.

"Thank you," she whispered, her voice watery as she gazed at Lolly.

Millie placed her hand on Abby's knee and squeezed slightly. "I'll share it with you at another time, love. I just . . . just need to let my old heart relax a little, okay?"

"But I . . ." Abby stopped herself at the pained look in her grandmother's eyes. "Okay."

"Being a mother is the hardest job God can give a person." Lolly set her teacup down on the table beside her.

"Amen to that." Penny stood and reached for Abby's hand. "Come with me, love. I'll show you what your mum left. Millie, would you like to join us?"

The three of them walked through the cute bungalow with Millie commenting on the decor and Penny making small talk. But not Abby. Her focus was on what her mother had left. She had a feeling she knew and couldn't wait to see if she was right. She fingered her mother's necklace until they reached the bedroom.

The room itself was charming, almost exactly as her mom had drawn it in the book, with a few updates, like the comforter and floor rug. There was a large window behind the bed, and the moment the door was opened, dust motes like old whispered dreams danced in the sunlight. She smiled at the thought . . . her dad had taught her about whispered dreams as a small child. She knew it was just dust, but she liked her dad's explanation better.

The back wall of the room was one large built-in cabinet with books and figurines.

"Is that a black sheep?" Abby asked.

"Charlie used to play with it all the time, or so Lolly claims. Katy plays with it as well. The sheep is her favorite. She likes to come in here, read your parents' books, play with her animals"—she gestured to a display of barn animals on one of the lower shelves—"and give me a few moments of reprieve."

Abby stepped forward and noticed that a whole shelf contained the Jack's Adventures books.

Penny pulled a frame off the wall and took off the backing. "We didn't want anything to happen to this, so we framed it."

Abby's hands trembled as she held the postcard in her hand. She turned it over to see a drawing of a traditional English garden, full of peonies and forget-me-nots along with daisies and other flowering vines that crept along a white trellis. She could see why her mom had picked this postcard for this room. The view from the windows was of the garden in the back, a scene her mother no doubt had drawn time and time again.

Tears gathered as she turned the card over and saw her mother's handwriting. This . . . this moment . . . *this* is what she'd come for. To deepen her connection with her mom. To learn more about her. To find the message she'd left for her.

She breathed in deeply.

> *My soul hopes to find rest here, like so many others, but I wonder if rest is not for me.*
> *I live with too many regrets. Too much heartbreak. Too many wishes and dreams never to be fulfilled.*
> *I might not have found rest, not for my soul, but I do see a way toward finding peace for my heart.*
> *That matters, doesn't it?*
> *With that peace, I would be able to relax, to let go of some dreams, to move past the one regret I will always carry.*
> *If there was one thing I could say to the child of my heart, it would be this: you will always be loved and treasured.*
> *My deepest regret is not being able to tell you that personally.*
> *But it's time to live past regrets.*
> *So this is me . . . attempting to learn how.*
> *Claire Turner*

Abby focused on the cursive writing, the way her mom signed her name, the rounded *C* and the way her *e* trailed off, all while she struggled with what she'd read. This didn't sound like the mother she knew. This didn't sound like the woman who wrote her letters, made her videos, read stories to her as a child through those videos. This didn't sound like a woman preparing to give her daughter the best life she possibly could without being there herself.

This was . . . it sounded like she was trying to say good-bye to something or someone. It sounded like she had no other choice but to let go of something in order to move on.

Abby was so confused.

"What's wrong?" Millie was there next to her. Abby handed her the card.

"That doesn't sound like my mom. Not the mom I've gotten to know," Abby mumbled. Her gaze fell to the rug, almost afraid to look up at her grandmother.

"Oh, Abby," Millie said after reading the postcard.

"She didn't know about me when she was here, Millie. She didn't know she had the tumor or that she might not live. If this was for me, then she wouldn't have that deepest regret." It didn't make sense.

"Love." Millie struggled with that single word. Abby could see it in her eyes. Millie held out her arms and gave a small shake to her head.

She went into Millie's waiting embrace. She didn't understand what the postcard meant, didn't see how it could be meant for her at all. This wasn't the woman she'd thought she'd get to know. It was not the mother she'd grown up imagining. This woman was someone else. Someone with a broken heart.

For one brief moment, she wished she'd listened to her father and stayed home.

FOURTEEN

MILLIE

Within the walls of the small library in their hotel, Millie embraced the stillness she so desperately needed.

Following their tea with Lolly and her family, they walked the halls of the British Museum, enjoying the journey back through time, before stopping in at an old pub. Abby ate fish and chips while Millie tried a plate of bangers and mash.

Abby was now upstairs, writing a post for her blog and watching a movie. They'd spent the rest of their day each locked away in her own thoughts and memories.

It was a lovely day. It was also an exhausting day.

After their afternoon tea at the bed-and-breakfast, Millie had to admit she was glad it was closed and that staying there hadn't been an option. Once Abby had read the postcard in the guest bedroom, they both couldn't wait to leave. The need to process what they'd read overwhelmed their desire to hear more stories about the time when Claire and Josh had stayed there.

Thankfully, Lolly needed to lie down. Whether she really needed it or was just giving them an out to leave early Millie wasn't sure, but she'd been relieved nonetheless.

Millie's fingers tapped on the postcard Lolly had given her. One that Claire wrote. For her.

It was hard, to read her daughter's writing, to see the words she'd written from her heart, even now.

Time didn't dull the grief. It didn't soothe the ache. It didn't shield the heart no matter how long it had been.

A mother shouldn't outlive her daughter.

She'd briefly scanned the postcard earlier, enough to know that, to really take it in, she needed to be alone.

Seeing the first sentence was enough to tell her that.

If I never see my mother again, I would wish her to know I forgive her.

Millie didn't deserve her daughter's forgiveness.

She was the one who hadn't stood up to Claire's father, her first husband.

She was the one who gave in and let him rule their lives.

She was the one who stood by while her daughter had to give up her firstborn son.

Before Abby had been born, Millie confessed one of her deep dark secrets to her daughter.

She'd kept in touch with her grandson through his adoptive parents. She'd kept that from Claire, and it had always weighed heavily on her.

Days before her death, she'd shared the pictures, the letters, and all the information she had about Jackson, Claire's son. She would never forget the tears in her daughter's eyes as she saw her son for the first time since giving him up. And so many times, throughout the years, Millie would see glimpses of Jackson in Abby.

She'd always hoped that when Jackson turned eighteen he'd want to meet Claire. But after her death, and with Abby's illnesses, there never seemed to be a good time.

She still kept in touch with Jackson, but it was mainly birthdays and Christmas phone calls and letters. He would be thirty-six years old now. His life was full. He had his own family and was content.

David told her that it was a good thing. That Jackson felt complete within the life he lived now, that there wasn't a hole needing to be filled. And she got that, she did.

But there was a hole in her heart, a hole only a relationship with Jackson could fill.

Millie refilled her cup with the hot pot of vanilla tea she'd ordered and looked at the postcard.

She needed to read it. Needed to read her daughter's message. But she wasn't sure if her heart could handle it.

"Stop being an old fool," Millie whispered to herself.

> *If I never see my mother again, I would wish her to know I forgive her.*
>
> *No one is perfect. We all make mistakes for the best reasons.*
>
> *I accused her once of not putting me first, but looking back, that's all she's ever done.*
>
> *She knew what I didn't—that I wasn't in the right place to give the child of my heart the best life possible.*
>
> *She knew what I didn't—that I wasn't ready for the responsibility of putting someone else first.*
>
> *She knew what I didn't—that my child deserved the best, and at that time, I wasn't it.*
>
> *But she was—for me. She gave me the best life I could possibly have. She's always tried to place me first in her heart, and even though she wasn't perfect, I knew she loved me.*
>
> *I wouldn't just tell her I forgave her. I'd also tell her I loved her. Now and forever.*
>
> *I am the woman I am today because of her.*
>
> *I wouldn't wish it to be otherwise.*

By the time she was finished reading, the words were blurry from the tears pooled in her eyes. She reached for her napkin and attempted to regain some composure, but it was hard with the way her heart swelled.

"I love you, Claire," Millie whispered. "I will always love you."

She caught the curious look from the waiter off in the distance and breathed in deep, giving him a small smile before looking away. She didn't need him coming over and being concerned about an old lady crying into her teacup.

Abby wanted to read this postcard, but Millie knew she couldn't share it. What she could share was the travel journal. Abby wanted to learn more about her mother, and Millie understood that. She really did. The growth of Claire's emotions, dreams, and desires were clear all throughout this journal, and maybe, just maybe, that would be enough for Abby.

Handing over the journal would be hard, but it would be another connection with Claire that they both would share.

Learning about her half brother, however . . . Millie wasn't sure Abby was ready for that. That kind of information should come directly from her father.

Which meant she needed to prepare him. Abby knew something was up, something that no one had ever told her. It was there in that postcard she'd read. She was bound to have questions, and Millie wasn't sure she could or should answer them.

The one question Abby had already asked left Millie at a complete loss for words.

Child of my heart—Abby had always thought these words referred to her.

It would destroy her to find out they didn't.

FIFTEEN

CLAIRE

My dear sweet Abby,
As I write this, you are doing what feels like somersaults in my womb, and I can't help but wonder what you will be like as you grow.

Who will you end up being?

Will you share the creativity and passion for the written word and for drawing like your parents?

Will you be so full of energy that you can't sit still for a moment?

Will you dance and sing and do ballet? Will you keep your father on his toes with your exuberance?

Will you fall in love with reading? Will you devour stories and one day write your own?

I dream about the little girl you will be and the young woman you will become. Will you have my smile? Your father's eyes? Will your smile light up rooms and your eyes dance with laughter as you catch butterflies and sing silly songs?

As you grow, I wonder what you will find interesting, what things will spark your imagination.

What will captivate your heart?

As you think about who you want to be as you grow older, don't think about what career you will have. Instead, think about what changes you want to make in the world. Will it have to do with child literacy? Homelessness? Climate change? Wildlife protection?

It doesn't have to be that big either. I wanted to touch hearts with my illustrations. I wanted to see the sparkle of wonder come to life in children's eyes as they looked at what I drew. Each and every time that happened, I knew I was on the right path.

I hope your dad tells you about Sami. She's amazing, and I fell in love with her the moment I met her. I drew her a picture at one of our book signings, and even though she's legally blind, she brought the picture right up to her nose and peered at every detail. I will never forget the moment she saw herself in that picture I drew. It was like I'd given her the best gift in the whole world, and wouldn't you know it—it was her birthday! Meeting Sami and seeing that smile on her face—it was another moment for me when I knew I had the best life a person could ever hope for.

I want that for you.

I really hope that I'm there to see you grow. To see your smile and hear your laughter.

In case I'm not, I want you to know that I'm never far away, that I will always be there, close to your heart.

I will forever love you. I can't wait to see what the future holds for you.

xoxo,

Mom

SIXTEEN

JOSH

The run he'd taken this morning hadn't helped to distract him the way he'd hoped. His daughter was in London, living out her dreams, while he waited for the proverbial shoe to drop. What had he been thinking, letting her tour Europe in the middle of winter? If she got sick again, he'd never forgive himself.

After a quick shower and a fresh cup of coffee, Josh was back on the computer, studying and analyzing Abby's blog posts, trying to read between the lines. Millie had sent him a text warning him about the postcard from Claire that she'd read and the questions she'd asked. He'd been waiting to hear from Abby herself, but so far, nothing.

Maybe she was fine. Maybe he was looking for something not there. Maybe he should stop worrying.

He wished he could just talk to her. She'd been gone for three days, and now she should be on the sleeper train from London to Munich. Her last blog post had been published two hours ago, three o'clock her time, ten in the morning for him. While she'd updated her travel journal with a few quick sentences, he'd been out running.

Abby's Journey: A Personal Blog

Trip of a Lifetime: Day Three

*Just stopped in Brussels before heading
toward Munich. I saw a Smurf, an actual
Smurf! Though Millie says I'm delusional,
here's the proof. Can't wait to see Germany
via rail—apparently we'll get a peek at lots of
castles. Stay tuned!*

*Millie is giving me a gift today. Can't wait to
see what it is—any ideas?*

There were a dozen or more comments already, offering various guesses about what Millie had given her, ranging from chocolates to a scarf to keep her warm.

She'd posted a photo, clearly taken from within the moving train, of a blue figure in a field. It was blurry and a little hard to make out, but there was no doubt it was a Smurf. The farmer must have thought leaving the statue where the train passengers could see it would be fun.

He should buy her one as a Christmas gift. She'd get a kick out of it, especially considering last year he'd bought her the cartoons on Blu-ray and found a boxed set of comics too.

They'd spent a whole weekend watching the cartoons.

He'd give anything to do that again with her right now.

Don't you think it's time to call your old man? He sent her a quick text message. He'd told her to call him anytime, and he bought her a plan so she could do that without worrying about charges, and yet . . . all she'd done was text or e-mail.

He scrolled through her Instagram account, looking at the photos of London she'd taken—of her smiling with Millie, of the tourist attractions you'd expect to see, and other random photos, like one of her passport on top of her luggage or a close-up of her train tickets. He wasn't too thrilled about her posting those last ones. What if someone were to see them and stalk her? It could happen. He'd heard horror stories on the news about stuff like that over in Europe.

He continued to scroll through her images, liking them as he went along, when he stopped at one in particular.

Abby and Millie posing beside a woman from the past. Lolly. Twenty years past, and despite a few more wrinkles and looking a little thinner, she was exactly as he remembered.

He could hear her voice in his head, offering him tea, chiding her husband, or telling Claire a story from the past.

She looked happy, but it was the pinched look on Millie's face and the way Abby's smile didn't quite meet her eyes that hit his heart like a fist punching into a brick wall.

Why had Millie taken her there? Why couldn't she have listened to him when he told her London wasn't a place for Abby to find out more about her mother? Claire had grieved in London. She'd left a part of her heart behind, and she'd once told him she could never go back.

He wished his daughter would reply to his text message. He needed to hear her voice. Then he'd know how she was doing. Until that time, all he had were questions, and they kept gnawing at him, and he couldn't handle it anymore.

Twenty minutes later, he walked through the doors of Last Call, where his buddy Mike stood behind the bar.

"So you finally decided to come see me. Took you long enough." Mike poured Josh a pint of beer and set it down. "Lonely yet?"

Josh took his time sipping his beer, letting the malt taste roll in his mouth before swallowing.

"A guy can only read through so many essay papers before he needs a break, you know?"

Mike snorted. "Sure, blame it on the papers."

About to argue, Josh stopped himself. No sense in lying to a guy you've known since your teenage years.

"How are your parents?" he asked instead.

Mike gave him a look, one that said, *I see you're avoiding the whole reason you showed up tonight.*

"Fine. Right," Josh conceded. "The house is too quiet, and Abby won't call."

"Kids. It's universal. I can't get my own to call either." Mike pushed a bowl of nuts toward him.

"Your kids aren't halfway around the world." Josh cracked a shell off a nut and flicked it.

He couldn't shake the feeling something was wrong with his daughter.

"No. They're an hour away, and I still hardly ever see them. You'd think they could call their poor dad on the cell phones I pay for each month, but no." Mike rolled his eyes as he filled another beer glass.

Josh looked around the bar and realized it was quite empty.

"Your dad would have your hide for drinking while on shift, if he were here."

Mike took a long drink and then wiped the foam off his lips. "Good thing my dad isn't here."

"He's good, by the way." Mike rolled his shoulders before he walked around the bar and pulled out a stool next to Josh. "They both are. They're quite the snowbirds now, although they should be home in time for Christmas."

Mike turned to look directly at Josh. "So what's the issue—other than Abby won't call?"

Josh rolled a peanut between his fingers.

"Everything sounds fine from what I've read."

Josh dropped the peanut.

Mike took another drink of his beer and then set it down on the bar.

"You're reading her blog posts?"

"Don't sound so surprised. The whole town is reading them. You should have heard the buzz this morning at the coffee shop, everyone oohing and aahing over her photos. Do you know Mrs. Greenwood signed up for that photo site Abby uses just so she could follow her?"

"I thought Bea Greenwood didn't even own a cell phone?"

"She doesn't. She's using her daughter's computer apparently." Mike stood. "This trip your girl's on is a big deal to this town. Want me to put something on the grill? I could do with a burger. You?"

"Sure." Josh wasn't surprised with the abrupt change in topic. Mike did that. He pulled out his phone to check it . . . just in case he missed Abby calling or sending him a text.

Of course, there was nothing. What was she doing right now? Staring out the train window at the passing scenery? Sharing a meal with Millie? Napping?

Found out today the whole town seems to be following your blog. You should give a shout-out to Mrs. Greenwood. She joined Instagram to see your photos.

Abby should get a kick out of that. Mrs. Greenwood had taken a liking to Abby years ago, bringing her homemade cinnamon buns and then teaching her how to make them.

He waited to see if she'd respond. But again, nothing.

"All right, the kid in the back is making us some food. Now, do I need to ply you with more beer or are you going to fess up?" Mike walked around the bar, picked up a cloth, and wiped the water stains from their glasses.

"How do you handle not having your kids around? Not hearing from them? Abby's been . . ." The words stuck in his throat like a soggy cotton ball. "For twenty years, all I've done is watch over her."

"Kids have a way of turning your life upside down, eh?" Mike leaned back and crossed his arms over his chest. The cloth he'd been cleaning with was slung over his shoulder. "I remember crying over my beer one night, and you and Derek telling me to man up. Remember that? You told me to find something to fill the void, that I was more than just a dad and ex-husband."

"Sounds like something Derek would say, actually," Josh mumbled. Yeah, he remembered that night. Remembered how lost Mike had seemed. Remembered how scared Josh had felt, knowing that would be him one day—and soon. Remembered how Derek had sat there, silent, without anything to say.

"Except he didn't say a word. You were the one with all the advice that night."

Josh winced. "Sounded like I knew what I was talking about. You didn't listen to my crap, did you?"

Mike snorted. "Funny that. It was good advice. Which you would do well to consider now. You put your whole life on hold when that sweet girl of yours was born."

"I had no choice." He shouldn't have to explain himself.

"Of course you did. Not many men would have done what you did. You could have let Millie and David carry all the weight while you lost yourself in your writing. You could have hired people to raise your daughter, but you didn't. You manned up, did the only thing you knew how to do at that point—love." He smirked when Josh raised an eyebrow at that. "A guy's allowed to go soft now and then. Leave me alone." He leaned forward, resting his elbows on the bar top. "The thing is, you don't have to anymore. That's what I'm trying to say. We could go on that fishing trip we've talked about. You could start dating, I'm sure—"

"No, man. Don't go there." Josh pulled back, physically distancing himself from Mike's words. "There's only one love for me. It wouldn't be fair to make someone else take second place."

Mike straightened and sighed. "You shouldn't be alone. Trust me."

They were really going here? "Seriously, Mike? Cause dating has worked so well for you?" One ex-wife, two broken relationships, and another on the soon-to-be outs. He was really telling him to start dating?

"Hey, don't be like that, man. That's a little below the belt." Mike turned and started fussing with the bottles on the shelves.

"Not everyone finds their soul mate right off the bat. You just gotta keep trying, you know?" Mike looked at Josh via the mirror, the pain in his eyes a stark contrast to the fake smile on his face.

"Not at this time, okay? And she's only gone for a trip. It's not like she's moved out or anything."

"Yet," Mike said.

Josh grimaced. The idea slithered through him like the chilly fingers of death. He hated that three-letter word. He'd heard it way too often in his life, and always in reference to Abby.

She wasn't out of the woods. Yet.

We haven't gotten the results back from her blood test. Yet.

She needs to live a normal life. Yet . . .

"You're not helping, you know."

When Josh eventually looked up again, Mike had his phone to his ear and held up his finger, signaling to Josh that he should hang on a moment.

"Derek, you won. I need you, man. Josh is here and in a mood. Help me out. I've got a burger on the grill for you, if you can make it here in ten." He handed his phone to Josh. "For you."

"You bet on me showing up here?" Josh frowned before taking the phone. "There's nothing wrong with me," Josh said to Derek. *They honestly made a bet?*

"Missing Abby, eh?" There was genuine warmth in Derek's laughing voice, and it quelled the anger that threatened to ignite when he'd thought he'd been the butt of some joke between them. "Tell him to pour me a cold one. I'm just down the block."

Josh waited in silence for Derek to enter the bar, and then he gave both his friends a stern look.

"It's not cool to talk about a guy behind his back. If you've got concerns, talk to me. Don't talk *about* me. And especially don't be making bets on me." He worked hard to keep his face deadpan, his voice low, and his body leaning forward. Derek leaned away from him, and Mike took a step back.

"At least give me warning if you do, so I can decide who I want to win, all right?"

It took a moment for the boys to realize he was teasing. They both broke into grins, and Derek slapped the bar top with his palm.

"There he is," Derek said, before taking a swig of his beer. "Come on, bring out those burgers, Mike. I'm starving."

Josh and Mike looked at one another. Josh arched an eyebrow as Mike only shrugged.

"How many's this?" Josh nodded toward the drink in Derek's hand.

"What? It's after twelve. There's no sin in having a beer or two this time of day, is there? And no, I didn't drive. I was over at the clinic with my beautiful but bewildering wife." Derek lifted his beer, as if saluting his wife, Abigail, before taking an extra-long drink.

"Bewildering?" Beautiful, yes. Smart, sassy, a know-it-all at the best of times, but this was probably the first time he'd ever heard Derek call her bewildering.

"She wants to go away. On a vacation," Derek mumbled.

"And?" Josh didn't see much of a problem with that. Derek and Abigail often went on vacations.

"I don't get why we need to."

Josh stared at him blankly, really not seeing the issue.

"She wants to go within the week." Derek's leg bounced, his pinkie finger tapped repeatedly against the table, and he stared straight ahead, not looking at Josh at all.

"Spit it out," Josh said. He knew his friend well enough to know that whatever his reasons for not wanting to go away on a vacation with his wife, if he wasn't saying it out loud, it must have to do with him.

"He doesn't want to leave you behind," Mike said incredulously, shaking his head.

"Leave me behind?" Josh punched Derek on the shoulder. "Seriously, dude? I don't need to be babysat."

"Really? Then why didn't you go with your daughter to Germany? Make it a family thing? Abby asked you to, wanted you to." Derek finally turned and looked him straight in the eye.

Josh blanched. A cold draft wrapped its thin tendrils around his ankles and wove its way upward until it squeezed his heart. Sweat beaded along his forehead, and the tips of his fingers were suddenly hot to the touch.

"Josh, you okay?" Mike passed him a glass of water.

Josh drank the water then handed the glass back for more. He chugged that one just as fast.

"Breathe, man, just breathe." Derek gripped his shoulder and squeezed.

Josh did just that—breathed in and out, focusing on the Jack Daniels label on the bottle across from him.

"I should have gone with her. She asked me to. I just . . ." His hands trembled, so he jammed them beneath his thighs. "I just couldn't."

"Don't beat yourself up over it. She's with Millie. They are having a great time. She'll always remember this trip. It's good for her," Mike said.

A bell sounded.

"Burgers ready, gents." Mike went into the kitchen, and Josh used the time to shake off the feeling of panic. He could do this. He could.

"Mike's right, you know." Derek turned on the stool to face him. "It is good for her. You both need this time apart."

Josh rolled his eyes. "I don't need my hand held. I know it's good for her. Why do you think I let her go?" He felt grossly inadequate. Thanks to this panic attack, his friends now took him for an insecure parent with a codependent relationship with his daughter.

"She's finding things out about Claire, things I didn't want her to know. Not yet. Hell, she won't even return my text messages or call me like I told her to. Why can't she just call?"

"She seemed fine to me." Derek frowned.

Josh frowned back. "She seemed fine to you? How would you know? Has she contacted you or your wife and you didn't tell me? Seriously, dude—"

"Whoa." Derek held up his hands. "Calm down, papa bear. Abigail sent her a text this morning after reading her blog posts and they ended up chatting a bit."

The blog posts.

"The whole town has been reading them, I hear." Josh couldn't help it—he smiled a little. Throughout everything, from Claire's illness, to her death, to Abby always being sick, this town had been there, like a family for him.

"You should have heard the talk at the clinic. People can't wait to read about the markets. There's a group of teens planning to go to London for spring break. Guess they're trying to talk some parents into going with them."

"That's my Abby for you. Inspiring others." He was worried, and now a little perturbed that she'd obviously talked to Abigail rather than him, but he couldn't help it—he was still proud of her.

"So she didn't say anything was wrong?" Josh asked.

Derek shook his head. "Abigail said she sounded a bit tired but excited to be heading to Germany."

"Tired?" Josh didn't like the sound of that. Was she not getting enough sleep? What about her sleep app? He had access to it on his computer, didn't he? He needed to check into that, to see how many hours she was getting and what kind of sleep.

"If she doesn't get enough sleep, she could—"

"Stop." Derek slapped his hand on the bar. "Just stop." His voice rose in volume. "Get over it. She's fine. Of course, she's tired. Her body needs to adjust to the time change. But she'll be fine."

"Get over it?" Josh planted his feet on the floor, pushing his stool back as he did so. "She's fine? Is that what she told you? That she's fine?" He leaned in, his finger pushing at Derek's shoulder. "She says that when she's about to get sick." That ghostly chill from earlier twined itself around his limbs. "God help me, Derek, if she gets sick . . ." He staggered back a step, exhaustion filling him within an instant.

Derek stood and placed his hands on Josh's shoulders, easing him back onto the stool. "She's fi—. Scratch that." He let out a long breath. "She's okay. Abigail isn't worried. She doesn't want you to be worried either. Trust me." He winced as he rubbed the spot Josh had jabbed.

A low agonizing groan tore itself from Josh. "I can't."

"Can't what?" Mike appeared and set the plates with burgers down on the bar. "What did I miss?"

Josh looked at Derek, who stared at him and then down at the floor.

"Come on, guys. We're not about to have another Turner versus Cox showdown, the kind where I end up being the only one with a bloody nose and a black eye? Cause, seriously, I've already paid my dues."

The edge of Josh's lips turned up at the memory. Alcohol. Bruised egos. Derek being a smart-ass, and for once Josh had had enough. Unfortunately, Mike stepped in just as Josh swung.

"We're not kids anymore." Josh looked over at Derek who had a smirk on his face.

"We weren't kids," Derek said.

They shared a smile before Josh picked up his burger and took a bite.

"Josh is worried about Abby." Derek waited until Josh's mouth was full—of course.

"I thought I got him past that." He took a fry from Josh's plate and bit into it. "Didn't I get you through that? No? Well, no need to be worried, bro. She's fine." He glanced at his watch. "What time is it for her? Close to dinner. Or past it, right?"

"Why don't you just call Millie, if you're so worried?" Derek said. "And what could she possibly find out about Claire that would ruin her trip?"

Josh set his burger down and paused.

A few things.

Abby could find out about Claire's depression.

Abby could find out the truth about who the "child of her heart" was.

Abby could find out about Jackson, the son Claire gave up for adoption.

The half brother he'd never told her about.

SEVENTEEN

MILLIE

M illie pushed the sleep mask up onto her forehead and frowned at the soft blue light coming from Abby's bed.

"Girl, you're supposed to be sleeping." Millie pulled the covers off and swung her legs over the edge.

Abby was lying on her side, holding her phone over the pages of a journal Millie had given her—or rather, loaned to her.

That journal hadn't been out of her hands since she opened the first pages on the train yesterday.

The worn, leather-bound journal had seen better days. The spine was creased, the pages bent, the edges frayed. The leather was smooth and cracked in places, obviously well loved.

As hard as it had been to share it with her, Millie had no regrets. The moment Abby saw her mother's handwriting, she knew. She knew she'd made the right decision to share it with her.

"I know, I know." Abby coughed, then quickly covered her mouth. "My throat is dry, that's all."

"Drink your water, then." Millie handed her a bottle of water that she'd placed on the table between the two beds before shuffling across the room and into the bathroom.

When she emerged, Abby was sitting up, the bottle of water half-gone and the journal closed.

"Throat better?" The last thing she needed was Abby getting sick. Josh would never forgive her.

It'd been bad enough when he called and blamed her for not convincing Abby to get in touch with him.

He'd quizzed her for a solid five minutes about how Abby was feeling: was she tired, cold, coughing, sleeping well, eating enough?

"Do you find the room dry at all? Maybe we could open a window a little?"

Millie checked the thermostat and readjusted the temperature. "I don't think opening the window is a good idea. There could be a draft and that dry throat could turn into something worse." Millie frowned as she looked her granddaughter over.

"I really think you should get some sleep. We've got a busy day tomorrow."

"Millie, it *is* tomorrow." Abby gave her a sleepy smile.

Millie glanced at the clock and groaned. "I swear we just went to bed, didn't we?"

"Hey, I wasn't the one up all night, talking on the phone. I'm pretty sure I fell asleep before you did."

True. Abby didn't even get on her computer to write her post about the long train ride. She had a shower and then climbed beneath the covers and was lights out, while Millie talked to David.

She missed him. She'd told him about sharing the journal with Abby, and he asked if she was okay with that, knowing how hard it must have been for her. Not once did he tell her to stop being so selfish over something so trivial as this journal. And she loved him for that.

"What's the plan for today? Please tell me we're doing lots of walking." Abby got up and stretched.

Oh, to have the body of the young that didn't crack and creak every time you moved, that didn't ache depending on the weather, and that did everything you asked without hesitation . . . like bend.

"You should do yoga again, Millie. It'd be good for you." Abby looked up as she was bent over, her fingers touching the ground.

"What, you see Sam do a few stretches and you think you're the new yoga master?" Millie shuffled over to her suitcase, slapping Abby on the butt as she walked by. Yes, she needed to get back into yoga, but after spraining her ankle last summer, she'd gotten out of the habit, and as David liked to say, habits are meant to be broken.

"Our tour guide will be here around eight, and then she's taking us to"—she pulled out the file she'd brought with all their travel info and flipped through the pages—"Füssen to walk through a castle, then on to some small-town Christmas markets, before coming back to Munich in time to walk through the markets in Marienplatz." Millie looked up to find Abby standing at her side, reading the sheet over her shoulder.

"Neuschwanstein and Mad King Ludwig. So cool. It looks amazing, and I'm really hoping there'll be snow there. Can you believe it's the middle of December, and we haven't seen any snow here? It's like late fall here," Abby said.

Late fall indeed. It was still winter. Which meant Abby would remain bundled up whether she liked it or not.

"You're following Mom's itinerary, aren't you?" Abby kissed her cheek before heading back to the bed, folding her legs beneath her, and setting the journal in her lap. "Thank you so much for sharing this with me. I feel like I'm getting a glimpse into my mom that I haven't seen before."

The journal she held was one Claire had started years ago, when they'd first talked about going to Germany together. She had pages and pages of suggested itineraries—of towns to visit, markets to see, places to stop for pictures, unique historical notes about things she found interesting.

Millie decided to select a few of those itineraries and fashioned this trip after them.

When she'd handed the journal to Abby yesterday on the train, she'd had a goal in mind. Not only would this journal share a bit more of Claire with her daughter but it also would become a legacy to pass down. There were empty pages toward the back of the book, pages for Abby to fill up with their own travel plans. Millie asked her to keep track of everything they did, places they went, food they ate . . . everything.

It was the least she could do for her daughter. For herself. For Abby.

This was one journal that Abby couldn't keep, though. She made that clear yesterday on the train. Millie knew it was a bit selfish, but she had to consider her own feelings. This trip wasn't just for Abby. It was for her too.

For twenty years, she lived with the constant ache in her heart for her daughter, of missing her completely, of never quite feeling at peace with the loss of her.

She understood it—as a mother—the determination to do anything and everything to protect your child. Even if that cost was your own life.

But as a mother, she hated that her daughter had sacrificed her life.

It was so complicated. She lost her daughter, but she gained a granddaughter.

After twenty long years, being here, on this trip . . . she felt a little closer to Claire.

She planned on holding on to that feeling for as long as she could. And if that meant reliving that previous trip through the journal, then that's what it meant.

For now, for these few days, she was okay with leaving the journal in her granddaughter's hands.

An hour later, they were down in the little dining area of their hotel, Laimer Hof. They'd arrived late last night and hadn't really had time to get a good look at the place. The night attendant, on the other hand, had gotten several shy looks at Abby while checking them in, which made her blush almost continuously.

Laimer Hof was small but boasted five-star service. Abby's one request while in Germany was to stay at an authentic Bavarian hotel. Millie had to admit that Justyna, their travel agent, got high marks for booking this place. Their bedroom was absolutely enchanting with its slanted ceiling, wooden dresser, and cozy beds that were each covered with a handmade quilt. The bathroom was even a nice size. The only complaint she had thus far—which didn't say much since they'd only arrived the night before—was the absence of a coffeemaker in their room.

But the coffee in their dining room more than made up for that oversight.

"Another latte, Millie?" Paul, the owner, appeared with a tray and set down two cups. "Abby, I brought you another cappuccino, is that okay?"

"Thank you, Paul." Millie breathed in the fresh coffee smell and sipped, enjoying the jolt of espresso.

"Help yourself to breakfast, please." He glanced down at their plates and frowned. "Would you like more eggs? You need to eat more than yogurt and toast. Please," he said, placing his hand over his heart, "let me make you eggs."

"Oh, I'm fine, but thank you." Millie was particular when it came to her eggs.

"Millie, I think Paul wants to make you eggs," Abby said.

Millie could hear the teasing tone in her granddaughter's voice.

"Paul, my grandmother is a little picky when it comes to her eggs. She likes them either over hard or scrambled and dry."

Millie could feel herself flushing crimson, the warmth creeping up past her collarbone to her cheeks and flaring out to the tips of her ears.

"Trust me, Millie." Paul half bowed. "I will make you the best eggs you've ever tasted." Millie's eyes followed Paul as he turned and walked directly to the back where their small kitchen adjoined the room.

"You'd better help me eat those eggs," she said, giving Abby a stern look. It had taken a year before she would eat David's eggs, so she had her doubts about Paul's ability to perform this miracle in a single morning.

Millie glanced around the room. It was charming and had about a dozen tables, half of which were already occupied by guests. Photographs lined the walls along with decorative beer steins and a few sparse Christmas ornaments.

"It's cute, isn't it?" Abby pulled out her phone and started taking photos. "You wouldn't believe the e-mails I'm getting from my blog—people asking where the photos were taken. I should have written a post early this morning while you were still sleeping." She bit her lip as she focused on her phone, her fingers tapping wildly.

"You're on holiday. Tell them all to simmer down." Millie smiled over the rim of her coffee mug.

Her phone rang just then. She didn't recognize the number.

"Hello?" If this was some telemarketer calling about some supposed virus on her computer, she was going to have a few choice words to say.

"Millie Jeffries? This is Jana Boldt, your tour guide." The voice was soft-spoken, almost inaudible.

"Jana? Yes, this is Millie. Everything okay? We're just having breakfast, but we'll be ready for when you arrive." She silently prayed that Jana wasn't calling to cancel.

"Wonderful. I hope you don't mind, but my son, Lucas, will be there to pick you up? I'm not feeling very well today, and just need to stay in bed. Is that okay? He has his tour license and often helps me with my work, so you will be well taken care of." The level of anxiety in Jana's voice rose with each word she spoke.

Before signing a contract with Jana, Millie and David had looked over her website, and she remembered seeing photos of her and her son and reading some reviews about both of them.

"Of course that is okay," she said.

"Oh, thank you." The relief came through loud and clear. "I will be okay for tomorrow, please pray. I have been looking forward to showing you our markets, so I'm much disappointed."

Millie smiled at her words. "Stay in bed today and rest. We'll see you tomorrow."

Jana described what her son looked like and mentioned he should be there momentarily before once again thanking Millie for being so understanding.

"Everything okay?" Abby asked just as Paul appeared at their table with a plate of scrambled eggs.

"These are perfect, I promise," he said before leaving to attend to another guest.

Millie eyed the eggs and then cautiously lifted her fork.

"Jana is sick, so she's sending her son to drive us around today." She played with the eggs for a moment, pushing them around on her plate to detect any moistness. She couldn't handle runny or moist eggs. Even the thought of them made her nose pucker and twist and her stomach queasy.

Abby shook her head and tasted the eggs first. "They're fine. I've honestly never known someone to be so picky when it came to their eggs." She took another bite. "Nice and dry, just as you like them. You'd better leave Paul a nice tip," she teased.

Millie pursed her lips but took a bite. She noticed Paul watching her from across the room, and she smiled, giving him the thumbs-up. They weren't bad. They were very dry, to the point of tasting burned, but she'd take that over moist eggs any day.

By the time Lucas arrived, Millie had not only finished the eggs but also drank another cup of coffee. Abby had her nose back in the journal, going through all the notes on where they were going today, and she even began posting photos of things her mom had written.

"Why post those photos, love?" Millie had asked.

"Just one more way of keeping her memory alive. Regardless of how long ago she wrote this, someone today will see it for the first time and not know it was written a lifetime ago. That reader won't know whether mom is alive or dead or how old or young—and that matters, you know?"

It mattered. Of course it did.

"Millie and Abby?" Lucas came over to their table to introduce himself. "My mom sends her apologies. But don't worry, you're in good hands. Are we ready to go? It's pretty cold where we're going, so I hope you came prepared."

Millie stole a glance at her granddaughter as Lucas was speaking. Abby sat there in her chair, slightly starry-eyed, while Lucas stood there—his hand was held out toward Millie but his gaze was focused on the beautiful brunette who accompanied her.

Millie could only imagine what was going through her head. She remembered what young love was like, when two people felt an intense attraction the moment they met.

She knew Abby hadn't really experienced the joy of young romance. Living the sheltered life she had, Abby hadn't yet fallen in love.

If Claire were here, how would she react? Would she smile and encourage this for the few short days they had, or would she step in and attempt to spare her daughter the heartache sure to come?

There was really only one thing a grandmother could do.

"Lucas, we are more than ready for whatever you have in store for us today." She shook his hand, ignoring the slightly damp feel. "Aren't we Abby? I have no doubt you'll make this day a dream come true."

Abby shot her a warning look, and Millie chuckled, because she knew what that expression meant. It was a cross between *Oh God, please don't say anything that will embarrass me even more* and *Yes, this is me rolling my eyes at you.*

"It's the trip of a lifetime." Abby beamed a bright smile at Lucas as she wound her arm through Millie's and pulled her close to her side.

"Behave," Abby whispered furiously into Millie's ear as Lucas led the way out of the hotel and to the waiting van.

"Why? We're on vacation. This is the time to enjoy every moment of life, and trust me, Abby, my entire objective today is to ensure you relish every single moment."

After all, that is exactly what Claire would expect.

❖   ❖   ❖

Two hours later, Millie was glad she listened to Abby about bringing her warmest mitts.

"I don't think I can feel my fingers," Millie said, working her stiff, mitted hands down into her jacket pockets as she shivered.

"Oh, come on, it's not that cold." Abby's eyes were bright with excitement as she stood on the bridge at the edge of Füssen and took photos of the cascading waterfall.

"This is probably one of the most picturesque spots in this town. I bring guests here to visit the Lech Falls all the time. You should see it as the sun crests over the mountains. I never take enough photos." Lucas stood off to the side, his own camera slung around his neck.

"*Lechfalls* means . . . waterfall, right?" Abby asked, completely oblivious to the number of photos Lucas had taken with her in the frame. Millie thought it was cute. If he took anymore though, she might need to say something.

"Right." The smile Lucas gave her granddaughter was almost too much. Millie shook her head at her granddaughter's oblivion.

"What time is our reservation?" Millie asked. All she could think about was getting back into the warm van. She couldn't believe how cold it was here. It didn't help that the ground was sheathed in mist, and you couldn't see the sun. She'd give anything for a mug of hot tea right about now.

"If we leave now, there's time to grab a warm beverage if you're interested," Lucas said.

"Young man, if I weren't married, I'd kiss you right now." Millie winked at him before heading back toward the van.

"Not to mention too old."

"I heard that, Abby," Millie called out over her shoulder. *Cheeky little* . . .

"I won't tell my mom if you don't," Lucas quipped back at Millie as he jogged ahead of her to open the van door.

Millie patted his cheek. "Just bring me to my tea, and we'll talk."

She loved the mortified look on Abby's face.

"Don't make me call David and tell on you," Abby teased, stepping into the van.

"Oh, honey," Millie said, half turning in her seat to wink at her granddaughter, "there's nothing I could do that would shock that man. Trust me on that."

Millie enjoyed the drive to the castle. It really was breathtaking— even more than she'd imagined when she and Claire had first talked about visiting it. The way the mist wove its way around the castle only added to its beauty.

"Mom would have loved this, wouldn't she?" Abby leaned forward and touched Millie's arm.

Millie placed her hand over Abby's, thankful for the connection they had in this moment.

"Yes, she would have, hon." Millie couldn't tear her gaze away from the castle. "Yes, she would have."

Claire would have loved everything about their day, especially since they'd followed her itinerary to the letter.

After the tour of Neuschwanstein, Lucas drove them along a highway through the tip of Austria and then back into Germany, where they stopped in Garmisch-Partenkirchen.

"Now, let me warn you," Lucas said as he pulled into a small parking lot, "this Christmas market is beautiful but tiny. It's probably one of the smallest ones on our list of markets in Bavaria, but you'll soon see why your mom added it to her list."

On their walk to the market, Abby kept pausing to take photos of the murals painted on the houses.

"There are a few things Garmisch-Partenkirchen is known for. The first is for its skiing. The 1936 Olympics were hosted here. The other thing, and this is what my guests love the most, is the fact that almost every single building in this town has a mural painted on it," Lucas explained.

"Every single building?" Millie asked.

"There are a few unadorned, but the next town we visit has some of my favorites. Oberammergau isn't known just for its passion plays and hand-carved nativity scenes, the murals are also straight from the fairy tales. Hopefully, we'll get there before it's too dark, so you can see them in natural light."

They spent just a little over an hour walking through the dozen stalls at the market. At least half were food and beverages, and Millie couldn't wait to try the *glühwein*.

Lucas bought a cup of the hot mulled wine for each of them, and they stood around a tall table enjoying the drink as it warmed them inside and out. Millie especially appreciated the warmth of the cup on her cold fingers.

"Every market we go to, you'll find various sellers with this wine. The most popular are the red wine versions, but some, especially in Munich, will have white wine. It's basically a mulled wine with some cinnamon, cloves, and a hint of orange. Each market will have their own mug, which some people like to collect. Every year they are different, and I swear my mom has a whole cupboard full. If you don't want to keep the mug, you can return it and get a few euros back."

Millie looked over the dark-blue mug in her hand. "I like your mom's tradition. I think I'll have to do the same." She inhaled the spicy aroma and then took a sip, letting the wine sit on her tongue before she swallowed.

It was a good thing she didn't watch Abby before swallowing—she would have spit out the wine if she had.

Abby's face was completely scrunched up, her nose twisted, her neck muscles as taut as cords as she forced herself to swallow the sip she'd taken. With a shake of her head, she set the cup down on the table and looked over her shoulder.

"I think I'll have a hot chocolate instead."

"I'll help you order it." Lucas took a sip of his *glühwein* and set it down. "Unless you're a young child, they'll give you one served with rum." He glanced over at Millie as if asking her permission.

Millie held up her hands and laughed. "Depends on the age limit here for drinking. At home, she's past the legal age. Although, I'm not sure you've really had a lot to drink, have you?"

Abby blushed. "Do hot toddys count?"

"Considering drinking age is sixteen here, I think she's okay." He winked at Abby. "Try the hot chocolate. You might like it more." With his hand on the curve of her back, Lucas walked with Abby toward a hut where a woman wearing a fuzzy red hat served them.

Millie enjoyed her *glühwein* and made a mental note to serve mulled white wine once they were back home and to include it in their own market. Why hadn't she thought of that before? They served warmed apple cider, so why not mulled wine too?

"What do you think of this Christmas market?" Lucas asked after they'd all walked around it for a little.

Millie glanced at the bags they both carried. "I think it was a success. What do you think, Abby?"

Abby held up her hands, showing off her new mitts. Alpaca wool. "Still think you should have bought a pair."

Millie wrinkled her nose. They were nice, but her skin was sensitive, and they felt a little scratchy.

"Is there anything special you're looking for?" Lucas asked as they made their way back to the van.

Millie didn't even need to think twice about that.

There was one thing in all the years of planning this trip that she kept saying she wanted.

A nativity scene.

She'd always planned on buying one for Claire, of sharing it between them, of finding pieces to add to the display every year. But now she could do it with Claire's daughter.

"I noticed there were no nativity scenes here," Abby said. "I thought I'd read somewhere that most markets would have sections full of furniture and carvings."

Lucas's eyes twinkled as he they approached the van and opened the door.

"Most markets will have some booths full of little furnishings or extras you can add to your displays. But if you're wanting a really special nativity scene, then our next town is the place you'll find it." He closed the door, rounded the vehicle himself, and then got in. He half turned in his seat and looked back at Abby. "I know of a carver who creates the best wooden figurines in the area. I promise you won't find anything better."

"That's the one thing my Mom really wanted to bring home from this." Abby leaned forward, her hands folded in front of her. She looked at Millie for confirmation.

"She would have loved this trip, Abby. Everything about it, she would have loved." Millie stared out her window and watched the scenery pass by, blinking back the tears. Memories of her daughter's face, the way her eyes would light up like starlight whenever they'd talk about this trip—it overwhelmed her. She saw that same look in Abby's eyes whenever she mentioned her mom and what she'd have wanted to do or had written down in the journal.

Sharing this trip with Abby . . . it was a dream come true. Giving her that journal to read while they were here, a journal she knew by heart—it was a gift so precious, so true—how could she have doubted it was the right thing to do?

It wasn't just her and Abby on this trip. No, her daughter was here as well. She could feel her presence, her warmth, her happiness here with them.

Millie wiped away the tears streaming down her face as the landscape sped past, the ache of missing her daughter leaving an empty hole in her heart, once again.

EIGHTEEN

ABBY

Hey Dad,

Munich. We must come back. Octoberfest—hello! You and Uncle Derek can drink all day while Aunt Abigail and I tour around—sounds like the perfect plan to me.

Today was all about fairy-tale castles (like on this postcard), eating schnitzel, drinking hot chocolate, and buying a nativity scene.

Yep, you read that right! Millie and I bought a nativity scene (well, actually, Millie bought it, but I helped to pick it out). We're going to add more hand-carved items to it every year—the carver here will actually ship them to us. FYI: Be on the lookout for a large package from here. We were promised it'd arrive in a few weeks.

I can see why Mom always wanted to come here. It's beautiful. It's welcoming. It feels like home—how is that even possible?

I'm for sure coming back.

You should come with me. I know Mom would love that.

I'd love it too.

Love, Abby

NINETEEN

ABBY

Abby's Journey: A Personal Blog

Trip of a Lifetime: Day Five

Hard to believe we're on day five. In less than a week, I've been to London, took a train across four countries, visited a castle, and drove through southern Bavaria. It's a dream come true, and we've still got another five days left on our itinerary!

Between my grandmother and me, we've eaten more cookies than is healthy (and both agree that none have compared to the cookies at Sweet Bites), ate way too many schnitzel dishes trying to find the best one, and have tried too many variations of glühwein and spiced hot chocolate than we should admit.

Someone asked yesterday in the comments about breakfast—check out my Instagram account for pictures of what a traditional breakfast here in Germany looks like. Meats, cheese, tomatoes, yogurt, and granola. Like, seriously, what a nice change from the sugared cereals I begged for as a kid.

I'd love to come back to Germany when the sun is shining, the blossoms blooming, and the houses all have their window boxes full of beautiful flowers. I'd hike the trails, visit the tiny towns dotted along the countryside, and take photos all day long.

Neuschwanstein Castle . . . for some reason I thought we would meander through the hallways and turrets, and I'd be able to daydream about what life would be like here. Wrong. Instead, I followed a tour guide and tried to listen to the stories he had to tell about Mad King Ludwig. Can you imagine building a castle with no guest rooms . . . on purpose? The man was a true introvert with the lifestyle of a king, and it ended up killing him. The castle itself is as beautiful as you'd imagine—despite being only half-completed. I would love to live in Füssen, with the castle and lodge right in my backyard.

I wonder how many people have gotten engaged here. With the castle in the background. Wouldn't that be one of the most romantic things ever? Note to future fiancé (if you're reading this): bring me to Germany and propose here.

Now, off to write some promised postcards before we head to another Christmas market.

PS. We can scratch "Eating lebkuchen" from the list. Not my favorite. Give me Sweet Bites gingerbread cookies any day! (Sorry to all my new German friends . . . I loved the bratwurst. That counts, right?)

"This isn't quite what I'd expected." Abby leaned close to Millie and whispered into her ear. She didn't want Lucas to overhear.

"It's a bit . . . clustered." Millie nodded, her lips pursed together tightly as she gazed down upon the old city square in Nuremberg.

Red and white fabric covered the rustic wooden booths that filled the square below, and you could hardly see the people, they were packed so closely together. The idea of walking among the booths gave her pause. They'd walked past the crowds to climb the stairs and get a view of what they were about to enter. For some reason Lucas thought this was a good idea.

He obviously didn't realize neither Abby nor Millie liked crowds.

It was a nice surprise to find Lucas waiting for them again this morning. Millie teased her about their cute tour guide, and it took everything for her not to blush, which she knew was Millie's goal.

He was cute. And single. And flirted with her. Well, if you could call the way he smiled at her, or the little winks when Millie wasn't looking, flirting. Abby wasn't sure how to handle it. It helped to know that she'd never see him again after today, but she had almost no experience talking with boys, and she felt that lack acutely.

She'd never had the opportunity to really flirt. Not in person at least.

Sam, Lucas is flirting with me. What do I do? Sam was the only one she thought to ask advice from.

Flirt back, silly, Sam texted back. *But keep your eye on the prize, girl. You're there for a reason, not for some silly boy who thinks you're cute.*

Right . . .

So ignore it then? Abby clarified. She could do that. She could focus on Millie and play dumb. It would make life a lot easier, that's for sure.

Unless you think there's something there. Then flirt back. Long distance relationships are hard, but they can work.

So don't ignore it? Abby was confused. So very confused.

Millie leaned over and read the conversation.

"Have fun, but don't take it too seriously." Millie winked.

Abby rolled her eyes and waited for Sam's reply. Sam's messages could take time, since they were written with voice-to-text software.

Don't stress about it. Enjoy yourself. Seriously, Abby. A cute guy is flirting with you while you're in Germany—talk about enjoying the moment! Have fun and tell me all about it later!

What a funny friend she was.

"It's almost time." Lucas lightly touched her arm and directed her gaze toward the Frauenkirche, the old church with a distinctive clock whose mechanism was signaled by a midday bell.

Abby video recorded the mechanical clock as it struck noon—there were moving trumpeters, and bell ringers, and then figures went round and round the seated statue of the Holy Roman emperor. From where she stood, it was hard to see what was really happening, but she planned to add it to Instagram later, and knew people would enjoy it in any case.

"Have you seen the one in Munich?" Lucas asked them after the display was over.

"Not yet." Millie shook her head. "We headed down to the Marienplatz to walk through the markets there, but it was nighttime."

"That's too bad. It's a nice one too. This clock was installed in the fifteen hundreds. The glockenspiel in Munich is to celebrate one of our most famous weddings. It's more popular than this one, and one you really don't want to miss." Lucas leaned back against the rail where they stood, crossed his arms over his chest, and gave Abby a smile that should be melting her heart, weakening her knees, and making her stomach do crazy flip-flops. But all she wanted to do was laugh at his obvious antics.

Instead, she smiled back.

"Should we get going?" Millie asked. She slid her eyes toward Abby and then linked their arms together.

"Don't give him any ideas, honey. That's not fair to the poor soul," Millie said softly as they climbed down the stairs.

"I'm not. All I did was smile." Abby made straight for the first booth that offered warm drinks. Her fingers were freezing.

"Sometimes that's all it takes. Boys are simple beings, Abby, especially when it comes to girls they're attracted too." Millie ordered a *glühwein* for herself and a hot chocolate for Abby while Lucas stayed in the background.

"Ladies, I'll meet you in front of the church when you are done. Enjoy your shopping. Send me a text when you're ready, and then we'll take a walk around the city, and I'll even show you one of my favorite places to take photos." Lucas winked at her, then he strolled off toward an outdoor café, phone in hand.

Abby looked around and took a deep breath. The booths were ranged in rows, with barely any space to walk between those rows. It was as though everyone was being herded in lockstep toward one destination—the end of the row.

However, Abby had something particular in mind. Like other markets, there were plenty of booths here with roasted nuts, gingerbread, tiny figurines, lace, dollhouse furniture, and souvenirs, but this was the only market where you could find characters made out of figs.

"According to Mom's journal, we need to be on the lookout for fig people. Apparently, they are unique to this market." Abby caught Millie's look. "What?"

"I know what's in the journal, honey." Millie pulled her along by the hand, and they threaded their way through the crowd. They slowly worked toward a few booths that caught their attention, filling their bags with homemade cookies, soaps, and even a few slippers. Abby snapped a lot of photos—of children eating sausage and licking mustard off their fingers, of the fig people she'd been looking for, of heart-shaped gingerbread that hung from more booths than she could count.

"Dad would hate it here," Abby muttered as she was simultaneously bumped from behind and elbowed in the ribs.

"David too. I've yet to meet a man who liked crowds." Millie shook her head as someone blundered into them without so much as a blurted apology.

"What about Mom?" Abby pulled Millie to one side, where there was a little breathing space.

"Abby! Your fingers are freezing." Millie grabbed hold of her hands and rubbed them, as if trying to warm them herself.

Abby pulled her hands back and stuffed them into her jacket pockets. "Let's get another warm drink," she suggested, looking around for the closest hot chocolate vendor.

"Where are your mitts?" Millie frowned.

Abby could see the concern on her grandmother's face, and she hoped the smile she gave her alleviated any worry.

The crease lines around Millie's lips told her otherwise.

"I left them in the van." *Yeah, yeah, stupid move.* She was ready for the lecture to come.

For a split second, it looked like Millie was about to say something, but instead she pulled off her own mitts and handed them to her.

A long, silent moment of staring stretched out between them. In the end, it was Millie who won.

"For the record," Millie said once they continued walking, "your mother loved crowds. They never seemed to bother her. She would take her time, not let anyone rush her. I sometimes wondered if she even noticed the people." Millie chuckled to herself. "She would have loved this. Instead of feeling claustrophobic, she'd feed off the energy here, take it all in, and then crash by nightfall, saying that being in the throng was the best part of the day."

They stopped at a booth filled with painted canvases.

"She would also find a spot to sit and fill a few pages of her sketchbook with drawings. There's so much here she'd want to capture." Wincing as if in pain, Millie turned away from the painting she'd been looking at.

"Are you okay?" Abby asked, concerned.

Millie nodded but didn't reply. Instead, she continued down their last row, her gaze focused on the church ahead of them.

Abby began to follow but stopped abruptly, her attention snagged by something familiar.

A booth full of sheep. Stuffed, painted, figurines, knitted, hand-sewn . . . everything and anything sheep related.

As if in a trance, Abby stepped toward the display, not caring that she cut people off as she walked in front of them.

"*Guten tag,*" she said to the woman behind the opening of the booth. "Do you have any black sheep?"

"Black?" The woman clarified.

Abby nodded. She looked around but didn't see any.

The woman nodded, holding up her finger. "I have one black sheep," she said. She turned and sorted through some boxes. Abby stood on her tiptoes, as if the extra height would help to see what the woman was looking for.

"I only have this." The woman turned and held a black wooden sheep in her hand. She held it out to Abby, who carefully took hold of it. It was quite solid but soft, the wool attached to the carving downy to the touch.

"Oh, Abby." Millie appeared beside her and took the sheep she held. "It's perfect, isn't it?"

Abby handed over some money to the woman and then reached for the sheep, holding it in her hands. "It is perfect."

In that moment, the crowds all but disappeared for Abby. There was a peace within her that seemed to grow, to swell beyond her skin, and surround her in a bubble. She didn't notice the people nudging her out of the way or the hubbub created by the crowd jostling around her.

She'd found a black sheep.

It might be a bit childish, but every time she found one of the sheep, it felt like a gift directly from her mother.

She'd grown up surrounded by the animal—from her baby clothing to stuffed animals to the covers of photo albums and journals, all with black sheep on them. Almost every one she owned had been bought by her mother or given to her as a gift because of her mother.

She'd found only a few on her own. Three, to be exact, including this one she'd just bought. And each one meant something special to her. Each one was connected to a memory of her mother.

The first one had been when she was ten. It was her mother's birthday, and Abby was home, one of the rare times she'd not been sick and in the hospital. She'd made a cake to celebrate her mother's birthday but didn't have a gift, so she'd begged her dad to take her shopping. They, of course, ended up in a gift shop full of journals and teacups and figurines.

Normally she would buy something small for her mom. Something she could place in her mother's office. She knew it was silly, even at ten, to buy a gift for someone who wasn't alive, but it didn't matter. Not then and not now.

She'd found a tiny set of black sheep made out of glass. They were all nestled in a small pink box, and she had just enough allowance to pay for it.

The second sheep was a stuffed one. She'd been in the hospital and felt stir-crazy from lying in bed all day. Dr. Abigail and Uncle Derek had come to visit, and she convinced them to take her for a walk. They made their way to the hospital cafeteria, where Abby had a smoothie while her aunt and uncle drank coffee. As they were telling her about her mother's fascination with black sheep—which began when she'd gone to Scotland as a teenager and helped feed small black lambs at the bed-and-breakfast where she stayed—a woman dressed in a princess costume happened by with a basket full of stuffed animals. Uncle Derek had spotted the sheep and plucked it out of the basket, placing it beside Abby's smoothie.

By the time they met up with Lucas, there was a skip in Abby's step, though Millie was starting to drag behind.

The walk through the old town was almost magical. They strolled through a market full of farm-fresh fruit and vegetables, street performers, and even passed a petting zoo with a camel. Lucas gave them an engaging summary of the history, but Abby could see Millie flagging. Millie had slept horribly last night.

"Lucas, I think my grandmother needs a break. Is the car close by?" Abby sidled up to Lucas and attempted to keep her voice low.

"Breaks are for little kids or old women with walkers," Millie piped up. "If you're tired, just say so. Don't be blaming it on me, kiddo."

Lucas glanced in Abby's direction, and Abby shook her head slightly.

"You're right. My feet are killing me. I should have listened to you this morning," Abby said as she rolled her eyes, thankful her grandmother couldn't see her. "Millie has a theory that you shouldn't wear the same shoes two days in a row," she explained.

"She's right," Lucas said.

"See. I'm right." Millie called from behind them.

Lucas checked his watch. "Why don't we grab a sausage and then head to the next market? You've got to try Nuremberg sausage. They're quite famous. The van isn't too far away, I promise."

Abby's stomach growled instantly, while Millie groaned.

"So, Abby, tell me, what is it you do or plan to do with your life?" Lucas asked while they waited in a long line for their sausage.

"Well, Lucas"—Abby smiled at the formality of the question—"I want to specialize in rehabilitation for children with life-changing illnesses." At his blank look, Millie gave her a nudge, prompting her to explain more about what drove her interest.

She told him a little about her own background, about her years in the hospital, and living a mostly sheltered life at home, and then she saw the understanding dawn in his eyes.

"That is wonderful," he kept saying. "Not what I expected."

Abby giggled. "Tell me, what did you expect?"

Lucas shrugged. "I figured you'd aim to be a famous online celebrity, making millions off your blog and YouTube channel from all the traveling you're going to be doing. Of course, then you'll come back here, and I'll be your tour guide. We can go into Switzerland or Italy or even France . . ."

"I wish." She didn't realize how that came across until Millie had a coughing fit. "I mean . . ." She faltered and looked to Millie for help. "I mean I wish I could earn money doing that—who wouldn't? What about you?" She needed to take the attention off herself, before the foot in her mouth actually went all the way in.

"Tourism is a huge industry. It's my mom's passion and now mine. I'd like to expand our company, bring on more guides, and make a real name for ourselves in the business."

"I think that's wonderful," Millie said. "You can be sure we'll tell all our friends about you and your mom and put in a good word with our travel agent too."

"I'll even mention you on my blog. I get a good number of hits, so you never know."

"Anything is appreciated," Lucas said before stepping up to the counter and ordering them each a sausage on a bun.

They ate their lunch and returned to the van. During the hour-long drive to Regensburg, Lucas told Millie some of the local history of the market they were about to see.

Abby half listened. She was more interested in reading her mother's travel journal, which had pages full of notes on the Regensburg Christmas market.

Near a cutout picture of the palace, she had written across the top of the page in bold letters: "CHRISTMAS MARKET IN A PALACE . . . an actual palace, Mom!"

"Thurn und Taxis Palace," she mumbled to herself.

"That's right." Lucas glanced in the rearview mirror and gave her a thumbs-up. "Not too many people remember the name. The market is located on the palace grounds and inside its courtyard. There's another name for the market, did your mom happen to mention that?"

Millie looked over her shoulder and winked knowingly at Abby.

"The romantic road market," Abby answered.

Her mother had drawn hearts along the side of the page as well as a rough sketch of the palace. She had listed a few facts about the market: there are fire pits everywhere, all the booths sell handmade or unique items not seen at other markets, there were branch-covered booths, live musicians played at this market, tours of the castle and grounds were offered, and a basket weaver from a family of basket weavers was always in attendance.

"Is the basket weaver still there?" Abby hoped so. It was one of the things her mom wrote a lot about on this page. She'd apparently done some research on the family, and written down their website, where their home and shop is (or was) located, awards they'd won, and how many weavers were in the family.

"Aha, you've heard of a well-known secret." Lucas winked at her through the mirror. "Herr Muller, or one of his sons, should be there. You must get a basket, if you can. My mother has a few, and she guards them against our cats, who like to sleep in them." Lucas tsked softly, which had Abby smiling.

The way Lucas spoke of his mother, it was obvious they were very close. It was too bad she was still not feeling well—it would have been nice to meet her.

"Can you imagine trying to bring a basket on the plane?" Millie wrinkled her nose. "We'd have to ship it home."

"What's one more package to ship home?" Abby leaned back in her seat and looked out the window. Off in the distance, the landscape was dotted with small towns, each clustered around a large church spire. Abby wished they had more time to explore. One week in Germany was not enough. Not enough by far.

❖   ❖   ❖

Five hours later, exhausted and freezing, Abby couldn't believe how much they'd bought.

The Regensburg market was beautiful, especially in the twilight when the lights flickered on and the magic of the season took over. The romantic road market was one of the few with an entrance fee, but it was well worth it. Booths lined the walkways of the palace grounds, the wooden fences were bedecked in evergreen boughs, and there were indeed fire pits all over for you to warm your hands—which Abby did quite often. It was a simple, cheery experience, to walk leisurely along the pathways and not feel crowded, taking your time looking over the wares and even chatting with some of the vendors.

Her mother would have loved it.

Nuremberg was crowded and rushed, with few smiles on the faces of those shouldering their way from one booth to the next.

Regensburg was different—quaint and friendly, where you could take your time, and everyone was smiling, laughing, and even dancing around the pits to keep warm.

Children played in the fields. Parents stood along the fences, their hands curved around warm mugs of mulled wine or enjoying a sausage while swapping stories and keeping an eye on their sons and daughters.

Young lovers walked hand in hand.

Old lovers strolled, arms linked, savoring their moments together.

Abby would have stayed longer if they'd had the time. But it was getting hard to be discreet about her sniffles. They'd hit her halfway through their walk along the grounds despite the warm scarf wrapped tight around her neck, the alpaca mittens on her hands, and the hat she wore snug over her ears.

The last thing she wanted was to get a cold.

Her father would never let her leave his sight again if he found out.

The ride home was a quiet one. With the journal hugged tight to her chest, Abby tried to sleep, knowing she needed to be proactive in fighting this cold before it could settle into her system. Thankfully, despite a few wary looks from Millie, nothing had been said.

When Lucas dropped them off at their hotel and helped to carry the bags to their room, he slipped her a folded note with his e-mail address.

"Please keep in touch," he'd said to her softly while Millie looked on.

Abby searched in her purse for a piece of paper and pen and wrote down her website address. "Here," she said, as she handed it to him. "I blog basically every day. Check it out." She gave him a soft smile.

He squeezed her hand before leaving, looking over his shoulder once before turning the corner.

"No pangs of missed opportunity? No soulful sighs over what could have been, if only . . ." Millie teased her as she unwound her scarf and hung it along with her coat in the closet.

"There are no *if onlys* here." Abby closed the door. "I want what my mom and dad had, what you and David have. I'm not going to waste my time on anything less." She'd be lying if she said she hadn't enjoyed Lucas's attention the past two days, but it hadn't been enough to turn her head.

She grabbed a bottle of water and slugged it down, desperate to relieve the dryness of her throat, but all the water did was flow through the barbed wires gouging deep into her flesh with each swallow.

With a glance toward Millie to make sure she wasn't looking, Abby winced at the pain. She dug through her purse for the bottle of pills her aunt had given her for the trip and suffered through swallowing them down.

"Headache, hon?" Millie asked, her eyes on the pill bottle.

For the first time, Abby was thankful her aunt had sneaked into her hand an aspirin bottle, saying it was for her travels. At first, Abby looked at it quizzically, but then Aunt Abigail whispered that there was no need to worry Millie and to only use them if absolutely necessary. Then she understood—it was full of cold medicine and antibiotics.

Her phone rang. It was Sam.

While her grandmother got ready for bed, Abby slipped into the hallway, her phone pressed against her ear.

"Hey, girl, what's up?" She made her way to the little sitting area by the elevators. She kept her voice down so it wouldn't carry down the hall.

"How was your day? I saw all the photos on Instagram, and Dean read me your updates and blog. A market in a castle? That sounds so amazing and romantic." There was a wistfulness in Sam's voice.

"It was amazing. We'll add it to our itinerary when we come back, okay? Apparently they hold concerts there in the summer too and there's a museum inside the castle."

"It's a plan. Now tell me about your sexy tour guide. Did you get his number? Did you play it cool? Break his heart?" Sam teased her, and it made Abby's heart so light.

"One day I'll understand what it's like to have someone love me the way Dean loves you, the way my dad loves my mom. Until then, I'll keep my heart to myself. But yes, he was nice to look at, and we'll see if he keeps in touch. You never know."

"One day it'll be your turn, Abby."

Abby pulled her legs up to her chest. "I know." She sniffed and then clenched her fist in annoyance.

"Abby . . . Are you getting a cold?"

"No." The word slipped out too fast. Abby backtracked. "Okay. I've got a runny nose, but in my defense, it was cold out, and you'd have one too." She knew that argument sounded weak. "Millie does." Why she added that, she wasn't sure.

"You're getting a cold. Are you feeling okay?" The concern in Sam's voice was crystal clear. Abby could picture her friend's face, the way her eyebrows would knit together when she was worried.

"I'm fine, Sam. I promise." Between her and Millie, she'd almost had enough of being asked how she felt. She honestly thought she was past that stage. Apparently, she'd been wrong.

"Go to bed, Abby. Get some rest. Your body needs the sleep."

"Yes, Mom." Despite the obvious sarcasm, she did appreciate Sam's concern. "I was actually headed there when you called, so really . . . you're the one keeping me from my beauty sleep," she quipped.

"Cheeky monkey. Take lots of pictures tomorrow. I can't wait to see them," Sam said.

"You're not straining your eyes too much, are you?" She didn't like when Sam held the phone right up to her eyes or when she leaned in close to the computer screen. The strain couldn't be good.

"Who's the mom now, huh?" Sam hung up before Abby could give a good retort.

Back in the room, Abby climbed into bed, but before turning off the light for the night, she sent aunt Abigail a quick e-mail.

Thank you for the medicine. Don't tell Dad, but I have the sniffles. I'll be fine. I promise.

She'd made her aunt a promise to never lie about her health. A sniffle might not be a big deal to most people, but Abby knew better.

They had five days left on their trip. She was not going to ruin her trip of a lifetime or Millie's memory journey over a cold.

"Millie," Abby called out, hoping her grandmother wasn't asleep quite yet.

"Yes, love?"

"We don't have to rush tomorrow, right?"

There was a rustling as Millie rolled over to face her. Millie's voice was full of sleep, but her words were very clear.

"No, love. Why don't we take our time, sleep in a little, okay? We can head to Salzburg around noon or later, so there is no rush at all. Go to sleep."

Abby let out a long, deep sigh. She'd sleep and pray that good rest and the medication would do the trick, that tomorrow the sniffles and sore throat would disappear.

She wouldn't let anything get in the way of enjoying this trip.

TWENTY

MILLIE

A bby was getting sick.

This is the worst thing that could happen.

Josh will never forgive her. She would never forgive herself. She should have seen the signs earlier, done more to make sure Abby was getting enough sleep, drinking enough water, staying healthy.

She'd listened to her sniffling and clearing her throat throughout the night.

She'd also noticed the bottle Abby had taken out of her purse before bed. The bottle with the aspirin label.

The question was, should she say something or let Abby pretend all was well?

She'd sent Abigail an e-mail last night while Abby had been in the washroom getting ready for bed. Now she reread the reply.

> *Millie, make sure she gets plenty of rest and lots of liquids. Her body might be exhausted from the time change. Head to Brussels early, and we'll meet you there as planned. I'll have David take care of the reservation change and the plane tickets. Keep me posted. Abby*

*is e-mailing me as well, so that's a good sign.
Guess this means I'm spending the holidays
in Belgium—won't Derek be thrilled!*

*Talk to you soon. You know what to look for.
You know how much she can take before it
becomes too much. The first sign of a cough
and you come home.*

She knew what to look for. Of course she did. She'd been through this too many times to count.

Pale face, but rosy cheeks. Sniffles. Dry throat. Bags under her eyes. Forced smile. Shallow breath. Loss of appetite. Exhaustion.

These were all the signs before the coughing began. Before the inevitable hospital visit and then the extended stay.

Last she knew, Abby was still asleep, thank goodness. Millie had sneaked out of the room an hour ago and made her way down to the dining room, where she'd eaten breakfast and sipped on her coffee.

"Breakfast will be wrapping up soon, but I have a plate set aside for your granddaughter for when she joins us." Paul refilled her coffee then placed a piece of paper down on the table. "I checked into the train schedule for Salzburg. You've got plenty of time still."

"Thank you, Paul. That was so kind of you."

"If you must leave Germany early, you can't not visit Salzburg."

There was a gasp behind Paul.

"Why are we leaving early?" Abby set her phone and purse down on the table, confusion spread across her face as she stared at Millie.

Paul grimaced and mouthed *sorry* to Millie before he poured Abby a cup of coffee and muttered something about grabbing the plate he'd set aside.

"Millie?" Abby pulled her chair out and sat.

"How did you sleep?" Millie searched her granddaughter's face for the signs she just knew would be there.

"I'm not sick." The determination in Abby's voice sounded almost convincing. Almost.

And yet, Millie noticed the tissue stuffed up Abby's left sleeve.

"Okay, I have a runny nose. But that's all. I slept well and feel fine. I took some meds last night that Aunt Abigail gave me, and I think I caught it early enough." She drank her coffee. "We're going to Salzburg?"

Millie nodded. "Of course we are." She slid the sheet of paper Paul had left toward Abby. "Paul already bought us tickets for the one o'clock train."

They'd arrive in Salzburg around three in the afternoon, wander in the old city and take in the market before stopping for dinner, and then catch a train back. It was a two-hour trip each way, and while the late start meant they weren't able to immerse themselves in a tour of the city as she'd wanted to, at least they were going.

"Don't downplay this though, Abby. Not to me." Millie needed Abby to understand, to be honest with her. "Your health is more important to me than this trip."

Abby nodded but didn't meet her gaze. *Figures.*

Millie leaned forward and took her granddaughter's hand, holding it tight. "I'm serious, child. David is changing our flight because we're going to Brussels a bit early, but I promise you this—I will not hesitate to take you directly home if your sniffles turn into something more."

"I know, Millie. But I'm okay. Please trust me."

The way Abby said the word *okay* triggered alarms in Millie's heart, alarms so loud that she was surprised to observe herself as she remained seated rather than rushing upstairs to pack immediately.

She should be calling David now and returning home.

She should be calling Josh and letting him know Abby was getting a cold.

She should be doing a heck of a lot of things right now and yet she wasn't.

Why wasn't she?

"I sent Dad a text this morning." Abby's lips tightened.

"Text? Not a phone call?" To be honest, she'd probably do the same. Who was she kidding? She'd done the same with Abigail—sending an e-mail rather than calling.

"I'm too chicken, all right? I'll admit it." She shrugged. "*But.* I did tell him about how I'm feeling. I also told him not to worry, that I'm taking the meds, and that I feel okay. I promised I would check in once we get back from Salzburg."

"You just didn't want him telling you to come home now, is that it?" Millie understood exactly how Abby felt.

"Or," Abby said, picking up her knife and turning it in between her hands, "maybe he'll be so concerned that he has to come see for himself that I'm okay?"

Well, now that was interesting.

Millie looked intently down at her purse on the floor, hoping to mask just how much that caught her off guard.

"I'm crazy, right?" Abby's cheeks flushed.

"Hopeful, maybe. Naive, definitely. But crazy?" Millie couldn't stop the smile from spreading. "No, hon, you're not crazy. You're a daughter who loves her father, and you're only trying to help him."

She glanced at the clock on the wall by the front door. "Now, if we want to catch the train in time, you need to eat and I need to freshen up. This face doesn't come naturally, you know." She finished up the last of her coffee and started up the stairs.

She would not worry. She would not worry. She would not worry. Worry didn't do anyone any good. Right?

So why was she worrying?

Maybe they should stay here, relax for the day, go to some museums, basically stay indoors, and then call it an early night.

She jumped when her phone rang, and for a moment—one embarrassingly long moment—she considered ignoring it.

But what if it was David? Of course, she'd want to talk to him.

Except, it wasn't.

"Josh, everything is okay." She didn't even give him a chance to say hello.

"She needs to come home. Now." His voice was terse and almost combative, a volcano ready to blow.

She needed to either calm him down or get out of his way. She wasn't ready to be burned, and burned she would be, knowing Josh.

"Millie, I told you this was a bad idea. I knew she shouldn't go. It's winter, for Pete's sake. You promised you'd take care of her, that you'd watch over her, and bring her home the first sign of a cold." He sucked in a breath and the sound of it twisted in Millie's heart like a dull knife.

"You promised!" Fury. Anguish. Worry. Fear. They were all there, intertwined until it was one solid emotion whipping inside Josh.

"I know. Josh, I know. I noticed it last night and e-mailed Abigail right away." She tried to explain but nothing she said was enough.

"You should have called me. Me. Not Abigail."

Millie swallowed hard. He was right. Of course, he was right.

"I'm sorry." She sank down on her bed, leaning forward, elbows on her knees. "David is checking into changing our flights."

"For today, right?"

The e-mail Abigail sent flashed through her mind. *You know what to look for.* She did. She knew the signs. This morning, there were none. None that should really concern her.

"You need to trust your daughter, Josh."

"I'm sorry?" He sounded anything but.

"Abby. She e-mailed you, didn't she? She knows the signs better than we do, Josh. She knows how her body reacts, knows what it can and can't handle." She stood, moved to the window, and gazed out over the red-tiled roofs that led toward a large park adjacent to Nymphenburg Palace.

"That's not the issue." Now Josh's voice was softer, calmer than before.

"It is. Give me a few more days, okay? Just a few more days. She's taking her medicine, and she slept really well last night. I'll make sure she gets to bed early tonight as well. It's going to be okay." She needed Josh to believe her, to see that it wasn't as bad as he'd feared.

"You say that now. But when she's back in the hospital, struggling to breathe, and close to death, will you say it's okay then?"

His words shredded what little remained of her confidence, and she gasped, her breath knocked right out of her.

"Of course not. Joshua Turner, you know better than that."

She listened as Josh let out a long, guttural sound and waited for him to speak.

"Has she asked more about Claire?" His voice was very deep, and his mood was dark and full of memories she knew he didn't want to deal with.

"Not since we last spoke. Eventually you're going to need to tell her. Sooner rather than later. I'm worried this is something she won't be able to forgive. And I really don't want to be the one to break the news to her." She hated to say it, hated the position it put her in, hated talking about it at all when she couldn't read Josh's body language.

Her son-in-law wasn't known for sharing his innermost thoughts at the best of times. She'd learned ways to pry things out of him, and when to back off, but it was so hard to handle these things over the phone.

"Forgive me or her mom?" Josh asked.

Millie blanched at the thought.

Abby idolized her mother, had her on a pedestal—which was perfectly understandable given her circumstances. All she'd known about her mom were the memories people shared with her, the letters, the journals. And they all showcased Claire's strengths, her heart, her love.

To find out about a secret only a few knew? To find out that a secret had been kept from her—it would knock her off the pedestal, and Millie wasn't sure how Abby would handle that.

"Josh, you need to be prepared."

"What if she asks you?" There was hope in his voice, and Millie didn't like it.

"Then I'll tell her to talk to you. I can be there with you when you tell her, but I'm not doing this on my own." She was adamant about that. "I need to ask you a question. Is there anything in Bruges I need to know ahead of time? Is there a postcard at the hotel there?" She thought about the children's book Claire had created for Abby. Claire made Bruges out to be magical, a chocolate oasis full of swans and canals and old stone archways.

"That was a bad time for Claire. She'd stayed in bed for a full day, and I'd had to coax her out of the room to see the town. We made a pact not to deal with life that day, but that was after she'd already written her postcard. That day she said good-bye to him." He cleared his throat, and she knew he wasn't finished. "She wouldn't even let me read it."

Millie's heart sank like a dense loaf of bread unsuitable for consumption.

"In that case, are you sure she left it there? Maybe she brought it home or destroyed it?" She could hope, right?

"No." She heard him sigh again. "I watched her hide the postcard between some books in the main sitting area just before we left. It doesn't matter. Someone may have found it by now, and no doubt they threw it out, but still . . . don't go, Millie. Not if she's sick. It's not worth it. Please?"

Millie glanced at the door. She'd been on the phone with Josh for a while now, and she was worried about Abby coming back to the room and hearing her conversation.

"We're taking it day by day. Let's see how today goes, okay?" She saw the handle turn and panicked. "Abby's here. Bye." She tossed her phone onto the bed just as her granddaughter walked in.

"I just need a few more minutes, and then I'll be ready to go. Amazing how time flies when you're on a tight schedule, isn't it?" Millie babbled as she rushed into the bathroom and away from Abby's probing gaze.

"Were you talking to Dad?" Abby asked, her voice laced with suspicion.

Millie took her time answering.

"Or was it David? Don't tell me you're homesick for your husband," Abby said, her tone milder now. She stood in the doorway of the bathroom.

Millie stitched on the brightest smile she could muster and, while reaching for her lipstick, looked at her granddaughter in the mirror.

"He's the one who's homesick for me. Home is where your heart is, after all and we both know I stole his heart years ago." She inhaled deeply and then let the air out through her nose slowly, hoping to calm her racing heart.

"Now"—she turned and crossed her arms over her chest—"tell me the truth, Abigail Turner. Do you feel well enough to go out today or should you be resting? Listen to your body, love. What is it telling you?" Millie asked her.

Without answering, Abby stepped back and out of sight.

"Abby?" Millie called out.

"I need to live in this moment, Millie," Abby reappeared, her coat in hand. "Will you live it with me? Because I'm not sure I can do it alone, okay?"

Millie's chest deflated.

"You are my moment, love." Millie pulled her in for a long hug and then let go. "But of course, I will share this moment with you. As long as you promise to communicate with me if you get tired or too cold, okay? We can take our time, enjoying everything, but only if you stay honest with me. Deal?"

"This trip is over after today, isn't it? I heard you." Abby frowned.

"Your health comes first. Let's see how today goes and how you feel tomorrow, and then we'll decide, okay? Bruges isn't going anywhere. You could always come back." Millie replied. She hated having to curtail their adventures and consider leaving Bruges out of the itinerary, but nothing was worth Abby's health and well-being. Nothing.

"There's a café at the train station, and if we're lucky, we can get a smoothie with extra vitamins. How does that sound?" Abby forced a smile onto her face before wrapping her neck with a thick scarf.

The memory of Abby's last hospital visit—of her lying in the bed, pale and almost cadaverous as they waited for the antibiotics to kick in—flashed before her eyes.

Millie swallowed, her jaw clenched, and deliberately pushed the recollection aside. Today wasn't about living in the past.

It was about enjoying the moment.

One didn't always get many moments to enjoy . . . Millie found that out the hard way.

❖   ❖   ❖

The Bavarian countryside mesmerized Millie as their train swept past quaint towns and the picturesque countryside. While she enjoyed the scenery out the window, Abby sat quietly beside her, poring over the pages of the journal.

Seeing Abby so engrossed, Millie recognized the expressions inherited from her daughter. From the way Abby's lips would quirk to the furrowed brow and the slight tapping of her finger against the paper while she read. Something was on her mind, she could tell.

"Can we talk?" Abby turned toward Millie, a serious look on her face.

"What about?" Millie kept her voice light and her manner chipper, but inside worry wound its way through her like a snake.

"My mom." Abby patted the journal on her lap. "I've read almost everything she's ever written, all her journals, her notes and letters, her books, all the guest posts she wrote for other people's blogs. But this journal is different. She's different in it."

"How so?" Millie had a sinking feeling she knew where this was going, and she wished she'd somehow prepared her thoughts about it before now.

What Claire wrote about—what she wanted to see and do, her dreams and aspirations, her notes in the margins of what she was reading or even of what she herself had written—changed somewhat over the years. But Claire's voice, almost all of the time, was vibrant and upbeat. The excitement she felt toward her topics is almost palpable through her words.

"There's a feeling I get when I read through some of these pages, like she was sad about something."

And there it is.

"Was she?" Abby asked. "I mean, I know obviously she had to be sad at times. She wasn't happy all the time, but in this journal and the postcard from London, I get the sense there was a part of my mom's life that no one has told me about."

"Oh, honey." Millie patted Abby's hand. "Women are complicated beings, and there's always more to us than we let on. Your mother . . . she was very creative, and with that creativity came . . ." She groped for the right words. "Deep emotions."

"Really, Millie? You're going to tell me my mother was complicated and expect me to accept that?" Abby shook her head. "Give me a break. Was there something going on in my mom's life you don't want me to know? She rarely mentions her dad—is that what it is?"

Millie's jaw tightened, and then she sighed and looked out the window of the train, trying to gather her thoughts.

"If it's not something you can talk about here, now, that's okay. But eventually, we'll need to." Abby said quietly.

Millie sighed again and looked at her granddaughter. She saw Claire's tenacity in Abby's gaze, her stubbornness in the lines of her smile.

"The subject of your mother's father is a hard one, love. You know that. He . . . he wasn't the easiest of men to live with or to love, and your mother . . . she didn't have the kind of relationship you have with your dad. Let's just say that." Speaking about her first husband was always difficult, even now. She rarely thought of him by name, hardly ever talked about him or that part of her life with anyone anymore. Except David, and even so, only when it was absolutely necessary.

"So is that what the sadness is about?" Abby pushed for more answers.

"He was a huge part of it, yes." Millie swallowed hard. "Tell you what, how about we discuss this and that postcard when we get back home, okay? Your father was with her when she wrote it, so he would know more about what was going on in her head and heart than I do." That was the best she could do under the circumstances. And so, she closed the topic and opened the journal on Abby's lap.

"Let's focus on our day, all right? What does your mom have in there?"

Abby gave her a long look, and Millie could see that she was none too happy with her reply. Finally, Abby heaved a sigh of resignation and flipped through the journal to the Salzburg section.

"Mom has pages and pages of Salzburg info in here. I don't think a four-hour visit is going to suffice." Abby turned the pages in the travel journal while Millie looked on. She was about to turn the page again when Millie planted her hand on it.

"This is the only page we really need to focus on." Millie's gaze ran over her daughter's handwriting, rereading some of the notes jotted in the corners.

"Old town? So that's where the market is?"

"Cathedral Square. And four hours is all we need. We can plan to come back in the summer and actually stay in the city, do some tours, taking in the sights . . . we'll make your mom proud." Millie patted Abby's knee and stared out the window. She'd enjoyed watching the countryside pass by as the train approached Salzburg. The two-hour trip had been fairly uneventful. Abby had slept for about an hour, while Millie had gone through the journal.

She'd been interested to see what Claire had written about Brussels, but surprisingly, she'd only had one page of notes. The market was a nice one, but it was the sound and light show on the Grand Place that Claire had been most interested in.

Winter Wonderland. That's what she had scrolled along the top of the page with a little illustration of a castle, Ferris wheel, ice-skaters, and snow falling. Her daughter had talent, so much talent.

Maybe after this trip, Millie would look into getting this illustration blown up, and she'd add this to her wall, where other illustrations by her daughter were featured.

"Looks like we're here." Abby straightened and reached for their coats, which they'd hung up beside their seats. "We'll have to look for a map, so we know where we're going. I can't imagine it'll be far though, right?"

Millie raised her eyebrow, and she just looked at her granddaughter. They weren't walking—Abby already knew that.

"Fine. We'll take the bus." Abby rolled her eyes as she stood and buttoned up her coat.

Paul had looked up transportation options for them. They could take either a bus or a taxi, but the bus was only a few euros. Abby had suggested grabbing a taxi and taking a tour of the city, but Paul reminded her that doing so would leave barely any time for the market.

So no tour. No taxi. Just the market.

They followed the crowd off the train and through the station. Off to the left were the loading areas for the buses, and they searched for the number one bus, which would take them over the bridge and stop right in front of the market.

The bus wasn't too crowded, and the driver was nice enough to announce the market stop.

There was a sense of giddiness within Millie's spirit as they stepped onto the sidewalk. The driver pointed them toward an alleyway before closing the door behind them.

Abby grabbed her hand to pull her close, and together they walked, arm in arm, down the street. The roads were cobbled, and streetlights in the shape of stars were strung along the lanes, casting a soft glow onto the shops and people as they walked.

"It's so beautiful here," Abby said, her voice a husky whisper as she took it all in. "I thought Regensburg was magical, but this . . . this . . ." Her voice trailed off, as her mind cast about for the right word to describe the ambiance of the place.

"I know." This is what a Christmas market should feel like, what her and her daughter had dreamed of for so many years.

"Mom." Abby looked up toward the sky, a sweet smile on her face. "It's gorgeous. Exactly what you thought it would be." She turned to smile at Millie. "We haven't even made it to the market yet, and it's perfect, isn't it?"

"It's perfect," Millie agreed. They continued their walk, following the growing crowd. They passed a large glass triangle covered with light, and within minutes, the market rose before them.

"How are you feeling?" Millie searched Abby's face. She seemed okay. No sniffles, no cough . . . other than her sleeping on the train, things seemed normal.

And yet, she couldn't shake the feeling that she needed to be worried.

"I'm fine, Millie. Just like I was an hour ago and an hour before that. I took more meds before we left, and I feel fine. No cold. No sore throat. No sniffles. Okay?" Abby adjusted the scarf around her neck, tucking the ends into her jacket and readjusted her hat so it covered her ears.

"It's nippy out. How are you feeling?" Abby turned the question back on her.

"I'm fine, love. Sorry. I just . . . your father is holding me account-able, so bear with me, okay?"

"I'm an adult. How many times do I need to remind him of that?" Abby shook her head and walked ahead, leaving Millie to stand there alone for a few seconds.

"Coming, slowpoke?" Abby looked over her shoulder, an invitation alight in her eyes.

Millie didn't need to be asked twice.

A large banner hung above the entrance to welcome people, but it was the huge Christmas tree, with thousands of lights strung all over, the plethora of booths, and the Christmas music that drew all the visi-tors in. Millie wasn't sure which way to go and so continued to walk straight, past the booths to their left and through an archway, where she recognized the buildings right away. This was the Residenzplatz.

They spent over an hour walking through the square in the historic center of town, starting with the outer ring of booths and then mak-ing their way inward. Abby bought some handmade soaps, and Millie bought the cutest cookie cutters. She also bought more bags of cookies than she could count—in addition to eating their fair share as they strolled.

In front of a group of freshly cut Christmas trees a violinist played carols for a crowd of people gathered round. Abby sat down on a wood log, sipping a cup of hot chocolate, and took a video. Millie stood beside her, enjoying her spiced wine and the festive atmosphere.

The music, the setting, the large Christmas trees, the illuminated castle up on the hill—it was all perfect. Everything she'd thought a Christmas market would be and should be. She loved the booths full of handmade or original items, loved knowing she was supporting a small business owner. It reminded her of the market at home. She'd taken a few pictures of her own, to help her recreate this in Heritage for next year.

She wished David were here. She missed him. More than she ever thought she would. She'd asked him to come to Belgium, to join Abigail and Derek when they all met up there. She also asked him to talk to Josh and see if he could make it. He might need to be knocked out for the plane ride and he might need a few drinks to even get on the plane, but with any luck his need to see is daughter, to make sure she was healthy, would overcome his fears.

Abby was one smart girl, she'd give her that.

They had a little over an hour before their train left, and her body needed to eat something other than cookies.

"Ready to head back? There were a few restaurants I noticed on the way." Millie squeezed Abby's shoulder as she bent down to whisper in her ear.

"Sounds like a plan."

They wound their way back through the market, moving slowly to absorb as much as they could.

"I wish we were staying," Abby said, turning to look back once they'd left the market. "Munich is nice, but . . ."

Millie knew exactly how she felt. She wished they'd come here to stay even for a few days, a few nights. It would have been nice to wander up and down the streets, to visit the other markets in town, and—she glanced at the brochure she'd snagged at the entrance—to visit the place where "Silent Night" originated.

"We'll add this to our list of places we'll return to." It wasn't just a suggestion, but a promise. A promise to come back.

"Did your mom mention in the journal any good places to eat?" She thought she remembered a few restaurant names in the margins.

"I think an Italian place . . . and we haven't had Italian yet."

Millie laughed. "That's because we've been in Germany, silly girl."

"Technically we're in Austria, and I could do without another pork-and-potato meal."

"Italian it is then. Any idea which way to go?" Millie looked left and right. They stood at a T in the road, lit stars hanging above in all directions.

"Looks like there might be something just up ahead. Do we have time to explore?" Abby asked as she pulled out her phone and showed Millie the time.

"As long as we don't dawdle." They made their way forward, and what do you know, it was an Italian restaurant.

"Destiny or what?" Abby winked as she opened the door for Millie.

The little restaurant was half-empty, and they were seated immediately, a bowl of bread and two glasses of wine placed in front of them, compliments of the chef.

After ordering, Millie sat back and relaxed, while Abby pulled out Claire's journal and browsed it casually. At one point, she laughed and pointed out the name of the restaurant where they sat, the same one Claire had written down.

"Destiny, indeed."

Their meal ended up being a little slower than expected, and they had to rush through rather than fully savor it. By the time they flagged a taxi, they were running late.

Thankfully, there was a long line at the station, with police double-checking everyone's passport before allowing them to board the train. They found their seats, stashed their bags in the overhead bin, and relaxed into their chairs with Millie enjoying her glass of wine before the train left the station.

Millie stared out the window, saddened that it was too dark to see anything.

Abby reached over and grabbed hold of her hand.

"Thank you for today."

Millie squeezed her hand in return, not having the words to say what tonight meant to her. She held her granddaughter's hand, imagining for a moment that it was her daughter's, while she let the memory of tonight, of the market and the sights and the sounds, suffuse into her soul.

She wanted to remember this night, this trip, forever. She wished it could be burned into her memory, every single moment of it.

She closed her eyes, feeling deeply content in her spirit, when the worst thing happened.

Abby sneezed.

TWENTY-ONE

CLAIRE

To be read when you're ready to be on your own.

Dear Abby,

Once upon a time, there was a young boy who fell in love with a broken girl. He believed that if he could just love her enough, love her deeply, love her completely, she would heal.

His love was strong enough to mend her broken spirit and that once-broken girl grew to become a woman full of love, compassion, and hope. So much hope that nothing could stop her when she set her mind to it.

Which was a good thing, because, sweet girl, that woman was me and that young boy who mended me was your father.

If ever there was a knight in shining armor, it was my husband.

If ever there was a man who deserved to be loved with abandon, it is your dad.

If ever there was one who gave his all in order to be his all . . . he deserves your whole heart.

I'm trying to picture what life will be like for you, being raised by a father who will love you more than life. It won't be easy. You'll feel protected, treasured, and treated like a princess, but I know there will come a time when you'll feel secluded, cloistered, and your strengths and abilities doubted. You'll feel like your father doesn't understand, that he doesn't trust you, or give you space to make mistakes. That might even be true . . . to a point.

See, I know your dad. I know his heart inside and out, and I know that his whole life will be focused on you.

If he's not careful, his whole life will be about you. And if you're anything like me, there will come a time when you need to step from beneath his protection and live life on your own, making your own mistakes, learning your own lessons, doing the things you've always dreamed of.

Will you do me one favor?

Will you forever remember that without you, your father will be alone?

That, without you, his life would be in ruins?

That, without you, he will have lost his reason to keeping looking forward, his incentive to avoid the trap of losing himself in memories?

Love him, Abby. Love him without limits. Love him with abandon and acceptance and honesty. Love him the way he will love you. And when it comes to finding someone to love to be loved by, never settle for less than the way your father loved me.

He was always my knight in shining armor. The one who loved me best. The one who loved me enough.

The way I love you now. Forever.

xoxo,

Mom

TWENTY-TWO

JOSH

Josh's heart was about to rip out of his chest and the *thu-thump thu-thump thu-thump* ringing in his ears was enough to drive any man insane.

He was going crazy. That had to be it.

"Breathe, Josh. Just breathe." Abigail was there, rubbing circles on his back, attempting to be soothing. But it made his skin crawl.

He jumped up from the couch and went to stand by the window, his hand bracing against the cold glass.

"This is crazy," he mumbled. *"Suck it up and just do it."* He hissed at himself. The self-talk did little to help.

"I can't do this." He turned and faced the group in his living room. First Abigail and Derek had arrived followed by David.

"No one is saying you have to." Derek crossed his leg over his knee and set one arm over the top of the sofa. *Smug little . . .*

"She's my daughter." Of course he had to do this.

The moment he found out Abby was coming down with a cold and wasn't coming home right away, he knew he needed to go to her, to see for himself that she was okay.

Stubborn brat. Yes, okay, she was technically an adult, and she didn't have to come running just because he said so, but—

He said so, damn it, and she needed to come home. Where he could take care of her. Where her doctors were. Where she had the best chance of fighting off this cold.

"Josh." Abigail stood, hands in her jeans pockets. "Derek and I had already been talking about going away, and after seeing Abby's description of her trip, now I'm kind of looking forward to going to Brussels. If she's really sick when we get there, David and Millie will bring her home."

"You can meet them at the airport. Take this time by yourself to work on that book of yours without any distractions," Derek said.

Josh looked toward David, but the old man just stood there, arms crossed over his broad shoulders as he leaned against the doorframe.

David gave his opinion earlier.

Two words: *man up.*

He was right.

But the idea of getting on a plane and going back to Belgium, revisiting the past . . . revisiting that particular piece of the past—it set off a full-blown panic attack. He thought he was about to die from a heart attack.

Josh turned to stare out the window again, raising his gaze to the sky and wishing, not for the first time, that Claire was here.

You'd tell me the same, wouldn't you, Claire? Man up. Do what needs to be done. Be the father she needs you to be.

Words she'd said to him in her letters. Words he'd whispered to himself late at night when he felt lost. Words he knew were truth.

"Abigail, is there something you can give me to help?"

Her eyebrows rose. "Give you? Like a sedative? Sleeping pill? Is that what you're asking?"

He nodded.

Derek stood and clapped his hands together. "Alcohol. We'll get you right sloshed, so the moment you get on that plane, you're lights out. You've always been a lightweight, so it's not like it'll take much."

"If he's drunk, they won't allow him on the plane, you idiot." Abigail rolled her eyes.

"So," Derek said, shrugging, "we'll get him halfway there, he takes a sleeping pill, and by the time the plane is in the air, he's sleeping like a baby."

"Well, that's one way of solving the problem." David pushed himself up from the wall. "Anyone for some tea?"

"Isn't it a little too cold for Long Island?" Derek teased.

Josh smiled at the exasperated expression on Abigail's face.

"Tea sounds perfect, David. Why don't I go put the kettle on while you tell these knuckleheads the plan we concocted with the help of your niece?" Abigail smacked her husband lightly on the shoulder on her way out of the room. Derek playfully rubbed his shoulder as if it hurt.

This is what he missed. The teasing. The ease between people who've known each other for years.

An uncomfortable silence settled among the three men.

"You know she's probably okay," David said. "Millie knows what she's doing. Knows what to look for."

Josh nodded. "I know."

Knowing that didn't alleviate the tightness in his chest. It didn't quell the fear that simmered inside, waiting to make itself known.

"She's my daughter, though. I don't care how old she gets or even how stubborn. Asking me to stop wanting to take care of her . . . that's not going to happen." He picked up a photo of her taken in the summer.

They'd gone down to the harbor to do a little fishing and she sat at the end of the pier, looking out over the water, completely relaxed. When she'd noticed that he'd taken a photo, she'd laughed and let her rod slip out of her hands by accident.

"These panic attacks, you've had them for twenty years. They're not going to go away now."

"I know." Josh sighed. For twenty years, he'd been able to ignore the attacks. Maybe it was time to stop running.

Derek stood beside him and looked at the picture. "I still can't believe she dropped that rod. I was thinking of buying her a new one. Think she'd like that?"

"I don't care if she does or not. *I'd* like it. She keeps wanting to use my Mitchell 300Pro." Josh chuckled. "That rod cost me more than I want to admit, and I bet she's used it more than I have."

Derek snorted. "Well, she's going to be disappointed in the rod I have in mind then."

"Which fear will you take hold of, Joshua?" David's voice, low but clear.

Josh put the frame down slowly and turned. David was back in his usual spot, leaning against the doorframe, arms crossed.

"Excuse me?"

"You heard me. We all know you've never gotten over losing Claire. Have you stepped a foot inside her office yet? Have you thought about living your own life for a change, rather than the life you assume Claire would want for you as Abby's father?" David stared him down, his face stoic, but the look in his eyes quite gentle.

Millie always called him her gentle giant.

"That's not fair, David." Josh wasn't sure he really liked the direction this was going.

"Not fair to whom? You? Abby? Claire? Your family and friends? I know life hasn't been easy for you. Hell, we've all been at your side through the close calls with Abby, so we get it." David looked toward Derek, who nodded before sitting back down on the couch.

"It always amazed me how well your wife knew you. What do you think she'd have to say right now, Josh?" David asked.

"That's an easy one." Abigail entered the room carrying a tray with a teapot, teacups, and two bottles of beer. "We all know what she'd say, don't we? 'Suck it up, Josh. You're stronger than this. You've got this. Do what you need to do to be the father Abby needs you to be.' Take your pick." Abby poured tea into a cup and handed it to David, then she handed Derek and Josh a beer each. She poured her own cup and sat beside her husband on the couch.

"You haven't answered my question, son," David said. "When was the last time you went into her office and spent time there, sitting at the desk with your computer, looking at the books on the shelves, remembering your past with your wife through the pictures and postcards on the wall?"

Josh shook his head and looked at the floor. Answering the question was pointless—they knew he avoided that room at all costs.

Yes, okay. He would rather live in the past, with the memories of his wife when she was alive, as in his dreams, than to use her office as his own, forcing him to face the reality, once again, that she was dead. Everything else in his life screamed out to him . . . that he was alone, widowed, with a sick child. What was so wrong with having one room, one whole complete room, left untouched?

So no, he didn't go in there. Even now, twenty years later. But he stood at the door every single night and imagined the last time he held his wife in his arms in there, the last time they'd made spontaneous love on the desk, the last time she sat in her chair, knees drawn tight to her chest, while he read a page from their latest Jack's Adventures book.

What was wrong with holding on to love? It wasn't as though it hindered him, exactly. He held a job, went for his runs, still wrote here and there, drank at the pub Wednesday nights . . . He wasn't a recluse or psychotic or—

Yet, he was a man living between his fears.

David had asked which fear was stronger. His fear of going to Europe, of living another part of his life—opening more of himself to life—without Claire, or his fear about his daughter and her health?

He didn't need to think about what Claire would say. He knew what *he* would say, and that, in this moment, was more important.

"I'm coming." Right then and there, he made the decision.

No one said anything. No one even looked at him. It was as if they were waiting for him to change his mind.

"I'm serious, guys." He took in a deep breath and happened to glance at his hands as he did. No shaking.

In fact, his chest didn't feel like it was about to rip open. And he could breathe too. Like, seriously breathe—without needing a paper bag to blow into or dropping his head between his knees.

David stepped forward. He set his cup down on the tray and gripped his shoulder firmly.

Josh refused to break eye contact with the older man. He held his gaze, determined to show the confidence he knew he needed to have.

"Good," David finally said. "We leave tomorrow." He moved toward the door. "I think it's time for everyone to go home and get ready. We leave bright and early."

"Good point." Derek stood and reached for Abigail's hand. "Considering how you pack, you should get started or we'll miss our flight."

Abigail placed her hand on Josh's shoulder. "You sure about this?" Her voice didn't seem to evince confidence in him.

If Abigail didn't think he could do this, maybe he couldn't.

Who was he kidding?

All the resolve he felt a moment ago drained out of him. He looked around the room, at the room that Claire decorated. The same furniture. Same picture frames. Same photo albums. Same candleholders.

But then he noticed the little things Abby had added throughout the years. The painted figurines she'd made for Christmas one year. The books she'd added to the shelves. The bookends she bought for his birthday this year. The snapshots of them, together.

Always together.

He couldn't imagine a life without his daughter in it. She was his world. His reason for getting up in the morning. For pushing through

each day. For not retreating entirely into his own little world and waiting, just waiting, till his time was over.

*Please come, Dad. It's magical. It's perfect, and I feel Mom here with
me, in every moment. Share those moments with me, Dad. Please?*

That was a text Abby had sent him a few days ago. How could he
say no? How could he take this moment away from her? The making
of a memory she'll always hold close?

He couldn't.

"David is right. He asked which fear was stronger, and it's the fear
of losing my daughter that scares me the most. I survived losing my
wife, because of my daughter. Without her . . ." He shook his head,
trying to build up his resolve.

"What if she's fine?" Derek asked. "Because that is a very strong
possibility—you realize that, right?"

Josh looked at Abigail. She nodded.

"To be clear, Josh, I'm only using this as an excuse to go on a trip
to Europe." Her lips quirked, and Josh knew she was trying to help.
"Claire talked so much about the markets and, hello, *Belgium* and all
its chocolate—"

"Sure, sure, that's the real reason you want to go." Derek shook his
head. "Come on, princess, let's get going. Join us for dinner after you've
packed. You too, David."

Josh stood at the door and watched while Derek and Abigail left,
with David following behind.

He was about to close the door when David turned around.

"I'm proud of you, son." David gave a slight nod of his head.
"There's something I've been meaning to tell you, but it's never been
the right time. Millie has told me about the questions Abby's been asking about Claire." David's lips tightened as he let that sink in.

"Millie thinks it's time to tell Abby about Jackson." Josh took a
deep breath.

"What does your wife have to say about it?" David asked.

"Nothing." Josh didn't understand where David was going with this. Claire had never said anything to him about how to tell Abby about giving up her first child for adoption. He assumed that either she didn't want Abby to know or that Millie would tell her when the time was right. Maybe that was a little naive of him. Or he'd just been so focused on Abby's health that everything else paled in comparison—even this.

When it came to Jackson, Josh stood in the background. He always had. This was something Claire had gone through before they'd met—he was her child—though Josh had supported Claire in every decision, even when he saw how much it tore her up inside.

The day Millie had admitted to Claire that she'd remained in touch with Jackson and his adopted family throughout the years was one he would never forget. She'd cried in his arms as she stared at the picture of her son. He had thought she would have been angry with Millie for keeping this from her for so long, but that night, all she'd felt was thankful. Thankful that her son was loved and healthy, and that a future that included him was a possibility she could let herself hope for, a desire she'd harbored in her heart for years but had been too scared to acknowledge. They'd talked long into the night about what that future might look like once Jackson turned eighteen and was ready to meet her.

"Claire's desk, in her office. There's a letter for you. She said you'd know where to find it, that it was in your secret place. She told me to wait until you were ready to tell Abby about Jackson. She wrote Abby a letter that she wants you to read."

That was a hard one to swallow. In fact, it went down like shards of glass.

Another letter after all these years, and it was for Abby.

"There's one there for you as well," David said, reading his thoughts. "Take your time. Pack light—and I'll see you at dinner."

The climb up the stairs took forever. He stood at the door of the office but couldn't step past the entrance.

What was wrong with him?

The idea of Claire leaving him another letter . . . he should want it. Want to read it. Need to read it.

He'd read all of her letters over and over, soaking up each word until he knew them all by heart. This could possibly be her last letter to him . . . the last message, the last *I love you*.

The ache in his heart swelled at the thought.

There would never be a last *I love you*. Not from her. Not for him.

Why was it so hard for him to walk into her study? What was it that stopped him each and every time he tried?

Fear, of course.

What did he want most—to read his wife's letter twenty years in the making, or to continue letting fear rule his life?

Claire had believed every moment mattered.

He could do that by making this moment matter. And the next. And the next one after that.

That's exactly what he would do.

He stepped past the doorway and into the room. He thought his heart would get torn to shreds, that he would keel over with grief, unable to handle the memories. But he didn't. He was fine. Mostly fine.

He pulled the chair out from Claire's desk and just sat there, hands in his lap. He could picture her sitting here, working on her drawings or one of their books. He could still hear her laughter—it was so much like Abby's. Same with her smile—much like their daughter's.

In fact, maybe it was their daughter he was now seeing here, sitting at her desk, legs pulled up while she typed energetically on her computer.

Maybe it was Abby's laughter he remembered hearing, not Claire's.

Maybe it was her smile he pictured, not Claire's.

Maybe it's been Abby all along. Not Claire.

How much did he miss, not coming in here? Not sitting with her each time she asked. Not sharing news or reading books or working on their own projects side by side.

He pulled open a drawer and emptied it of all the papers and other knickknacks Abby had stored in there and felt for a little latch at the back, something easily missed unless you knew what to look for. The bottom of the drawer lifted slightly, enough for him to hook his finger underneath and pull it out completely.

There rested two letters. One for Abby and the other for him.

How much did he miss?

So much.

TWENTY-THREE

ABBY

Hey Dad,

Do you remember De Vier Winden—serving waffles and hot chocolate—where you and Mom sat almost every morning when you were here in Bruges? Yep. Still here. Mom said they were the best Belgium waffles she'd ever eaten. I'm happy to say the same. Did you know they sell their waffle mix? Guess what we'll be having for breakfast for a while? I kind of bought more than I should have . . .

Millie and I toured around the old city in a horse-drawn carriage. Don't worry—we were wrapped in blankets and had hand warmers in our mitts. Such a beautiful town. And, the market . . . so cute. There's a skating rink in the middle of the market square, Dad. You betcha I was on there too—so much fun! Millie loaded up on a few things, and I'm bringing home some small paintings.

See you soon! Really missing you.

Love, Abby

TWENTY-FOUR

ABBY

Abby's Journey: A Personal Blog

> *Trip of a Lifetime: Day Seven*
>
> *All fairy tales come to an end. Right?*
>
> *You know that feeling when everything is so magical, when life couldn't get any better, that feeling when you know, you just know, that something could go wrong, but you hope and pray it won't?*
>
> *Yeah. My happily-ever-after trip of a lifetime just turned into a nightmare.*
>
> *I'm getting a cold.*
>
> *To most people, that's no big deal. Sure, it sucks to come down with a cold when you're on vacation, but it's manageable. Right?*

If you're reading this post, then you know I'm not most people. I had hopes—no, scratch that—I had dreams that I could live an ordinary life, that for once everything would be fine.

I should have known better.

Don't get me wrong. I'm not bitter or angry or brokenhearted. This is the way of my life. I get a cold, and it turns into something worse—that is always how it happens for me. I'm just thankful that right now, it's just the beginning of a cold and maybe, just maybe, it'll stay that way.

Our trip to Germany to see the markets has been amazing, and one day I hope to come back.

Scratch that. One day I will come back. But in the spring, summer, or fall. Not winter. Next winter, I'll head to some place tropical.

Now, off to write some promised postcards before our last market, and then we're coming home. See you all soon.

PS. We can cross "eating a Belgium waffle in Belgium" off the list. So good. Like, seriously . . . so good!

Abby felt sick. Sick to her stomach. Sick in her soul.

How could this have happened?

She lost her mother's journal.

While Millie had gone for coffee, Abby had ransacked their hotel room, searching through all their bags, suitcases, and every single purchase—and come up empty.

She rubbed her face with a nervous panic. *Where could it be?*

She pushed herself up off the floor, where she'd just torn apart her suitcase and looked through all the bags from yesterday, again. Surely, it had to be in there.

It had to be in there.

Ten bags later and no journal.

Her hands shook. Her heart raced. She couldn't sit still.

Millie was going to kill her. Well, not literally, but she was going to be crushed.

Maybe she should look through everything again. She still had time. After their short walk following breakfast, Abby had gone back to their room to lie down, while Millie sat at a café just across the street and people watched. Abby had slept poorly last night and their walk today had left her slightly winded—although she didn't tell Millie that. They were leaving for home tomorrow, and Abby wanted today to be perfect for Millie.

Her getting sick didn't need to ruin things. Not today. They still had the market to visit tonight, and if Millie knew how bad Abby actually felt, she would veto that plan.

Abby hated lying to her, but they'd already been forced to cut their trip short because of her. She wasn't about to ruin their last day as well.

But then again, once Millie found out about the missing journal, that would probably happen anyways.

Her nausea churned anew at the thought.

There was a sound at the door. She listened as a card slid into the lock, clicked into place, and the door handle opened.

Abby tried to wipe away the tears that suddenly streamed down her face, but she wasn't fast enough.

"Honey, what's wrong?" Millie set her coffee down on the table and rushed over, enveloping her in a warm hug.

Abby tried to explain, but her words came out in a jumble as she tried to speak through her sobs.

"*Shhh.* It's okay." Millie rubbed her back and rocked her slowly. Millie placed her hand against Abby's forehead.

"You're burning up. Oh, Abby, honey, I didn't realize . . ." She pulled away slightly and looked Abby in the eyes.

Abby dropped her gaze.

"Did you have this fever earlier or since you woke up from your nap?" Millie's voice wobbled slightly.

Abby cleared her throat, forgetting her goal was to hide her symptoms as long as she could.

"Abigail Turner . . ."

"It doesn't matter, not really. I . . ." Abby sighed as more tears welled up in her eyes and ran down her cheeks. "Millie, I'm so sorry . . . I've looked everywhere but I can't find it."

"Is that the reason for the mess?" Millie glanced around at the disarray in their room.

"I lost it. I lost it, Millie. I'm so sorry," Abby wiped at the tears that clung to her cheeks before looking her grandmother in the eyes.

"What did you lose?" Millie handed her a tissue.

"The journal."

Millie pulled back, her face a mask, completely unreadable.

Abby scanned her face—looking for signs she was upset or understanding or something else—but there was nothing. That scared her more than anything.

She reached for Millie's hands and squeezed tight. "I'm so sorry, Millie. I'm so sorry."

It took a bit. Millie blinked a few times, and then she stood. "You didn't lose it. Is that what's gotten you into a panic? The journal?"

"I know how much it means to you. You trusted me with it, and I . . ."

Abby watched helplessly while Millie started to go through the bags she'd already combed through more than once, repacking all the items, scrutinizing everything carefully. For a few moments she held on to that glimmer of hope that maybe she'd overlooked it. Maybe Millie would find it. Maybe Abby was just so tired that she didn't see it.

Millie was saying something to her, but Abby wasn't listening. She mentally recounted their steps. She'd read it on the train to Salzburg. They ate at the restaurant her mom had mentioned in the journal, then stuffed it in her bag before rushing out to catch a cab. She fell asleep on the train, and the next morning after sleeping in, they hurried to make their flight to Brussels.

"Salzburg." Abby winced at the jolt that ran through Millie. "That's where I had it last. At the restaurant. Millie, we should call there, and see if they still have it. They must! They can send it to us."

Millie rubbed her face before she came to sit on the bed, reaching for her hands, her hold strong. "Oh, Abby."

Two simple words yet they carried the full weight of Millie's disappointment. The crushing sensation within Abby's heart was almost too much.

"I'm sorry, Millie." She placed her arms around her grandmother and held on tight, hoping Millie believed her. "I know you trusted me to keep the journal safe, and I didn't. I'm so sorry."

Abby stared into her grandmother's face and waited. Waited for the understanding to show in her eyes. Waited for the first hint of forgiveness. She would wait forever if she needed to.

Abby could count on one hand the number of times she'd disappointed her grandmother to this degree.

Each of those times, the disappointment was centered on Abby and her trying to hide being sick.

None of those times compared to this, though.

This time Abby broke a promise, betrayed a trust, and her heart hurt more than she thought possible.

"Abigail Turner." Millie's voice was stern as she pulled away. "Have you not heard a single word I've said?" She felt Abby's forehead again. "Sweet heavens, you're even hotter now than before. We need to bring your fever down."

Abby rested her head on her grandmother's shoulder. "I'm okay, Millie. Honestly. Just a little tired and maybe thirsty. Do we have any more bottles of water?" she asked.

"Abigail, would you please listen to me?" Millie released her hold, and Abby stayed where she was while Millie got a bottle of water from the small hotel refrigerator and grabbed the bottle of pills on the way back to Abby. She shook a few pills into her hand. "Take these, please. They'll help with your fever. I want you to take a tepid bath too. Cool your body down. And then it's back to bed for you."

"I'll have a bath later. Right now we need to call the restaurant." She reached for the clean tissue she kept tucked in her sleeve and wiped her nose. "I'm so sorry, Millie." She'd continue to apologize as long as necessary.

"How long have you been feeling this way, Abby?" Millie studied her closely.

Abby shook her head. "Millie, did you hear me?"

She'd expected Millie to be upset, to be heartbroken, and try to mask her feelings. But it was almost as if Millie wasn't even listening to her, ignoring everything she'd been saying about the journal.

"I heard you, honey, but I don't think you're hearing me. I know you thought you lost the journal. I know you're sorry. We'll deal with that because I can see you're fixated on it. But first, I need you to answer me. You seemed fine earlier, a little tired, but okay. Were you?"

Abby nodded. "I was fine. A little tired, like I told you. But I'm okay."

Millie shook her head. "No, you were okay, but now you're not." Her lips thinned. "I should have paid more attention," she said softly, as if to herself, but Abby heard.

"You came back to the room and lay down right away, right? Did you take any more cold medicine before you fell asleep? How did you sleep? Have you been tracking with your sleep app?" Millie fired off her questions in a way that made Abby dizzy.

"No, I just fell asleep. I took the cold medicine before we went for breakfast. And no, I haven't been tracking, I should have, though." She swallowed and flinched at the rawness of her throat. It hadn't been like that when she woke up.

"I didn't sleep well. I had a dream that someone ripped the journal from my hands and tore all the pages out while we were on the train, so I woke up in somewhat of a panic."

Millie nodded once, then frowned. "No doubt, especially with that fever of yours. Abigail, listen to me. You did not lose the journal. That was just a dream. I have it."

Abby didn't just hear what she thought she heard, did she?

Millie had the journal?

"You gave it to me, Abby. You obviously don't remember that." Millie's voice was soft, patient, as if explaining a simple concept to a small child.

"No I didn't." Abby didn't remember that at all.

"You did. Just before you came to lie down. I thought I would refresh my memory of what your mom had written about Brussels. There was a hidden-gems walking tour she'd described, and I wanted to see if any of the spots were close by. You don't remember that? Honestly?"

Abby shook her head, confusion clouding all her thoughts. Why didn't she remember that? She should have.

"It's okay, love." The look in Millie's eyes said more than her words did.

Abby understood that look. She'd seen it many times. Too many times to count.

"I'm really sick, aren't I?" Abby said. Why she asked the question, she didn't know. She knew she was sick. She thought she was handling it, that the medicine Abigail gave her was helping. But she knew the signs.

The exhaustion.

The sudden onslaught of her fever.

The confusion and fear and panic . . .

"Let's get that bath ready, okay? We'll get your fever down, get some rest, and maybe we'll catch it in time." Millie turned toward the bathroom, which had a large soaker tub. Abby listened as Millie ran the water.

She reached for her phone and did the one thing she should have done a long time ago.

Abby called her father.

She hated having to tell him she was sick. Sicker than she thought she would be. He'll want her on the next available flight, but since they were leaving tomorrow, she'll just rest today. That will help more than anything else.

She listened as the phone rang and couldn't believe when he didn't pick up.

He always picked up.

"Dad," her voice was a little shaky as she left him a message. "Please call me. I'm . . . I'm not feeling that well. I love you."

She sent him a text asking him to call as soon as he could.

She pushed back the tears. She needed to stop crying. Her eyes were now sore, and the headache that always appeared after she cried was in full force.

"Bath is ready. You go soak in there for a little bit, okay? I'll call room service and see if they have some soup they can bring up for you. You need your energy."

"Millie, I'm sorry." Abby said. Again.

Millie shook her head. "Oh no you don't. You're not going to apologize for getting sick. I should have known better. I should have listened to your father." She frowned. "Don't you dare tell him that, though."

Abby smiled at that. "I won't say a word. And this isn't your fault. I was fine before we came. It's only been the past few days, and honestly, there was nothing I could have done or that I shouldn't have done. Remember what Aunt Abigail said the last time I got sick? There's only so much prevention we can do. Sometimes our bodies have the final say."

She should call her aunt. Maybe Millie will call while she has a bath.

She paused in the doorway to the bathroom and looked at her grandmother, who was tidying up around the room.

"Millie, I love you."

Millie looked up, a sweet smile on her face. "I love you too. Now go on, go have that bath."

"I need you to promise me something," Abby said.

"What's that?"

"I'll go take a bath and then crawl into bed and watch some movies on my computer. But"—she gave her grandmother a stern look—"I want you to promise that you'll go out and enjoy the city." She glanced at the clock between the beds. "I happen to know there is a walking tour starting in thirty minutes, and all you need to do is contact the concierge and they'll make sure the group doesn't leave without you."

Millie snorted. "Really? And you know this how?"

Abby nodded toward a little pile of papers and brochures from the hotel, which she'd left on the writing desk in the corner.

Millie read through it, then looked at her watch and back at the sheet.

"That does sound like fun, doesn't it?" Millie mused.

"It does. And I promise not to leave this room."

Millie shook her head. "I'm not about to leave you when you're not well. I never have before, and I won't start now."

"I'm an adult, Millie. I can take care of myself for a few hours." She omitted the fact that she was both dizzy and exhausted.

"Go have that bath. I'll be here." She sat down in the corner chair and reached for one of the books Millie always kept with her.

"Are you sure? I feel bad that you are staying here when you could be out enjoying yourself." She closed the door and got ready for the bath, testing it with her hands first. She knew from experience that no matter the temperature of the bath, if her body was hot enough, it would always feel frigid.

A few minutes into her bath, there was a knock on the door.

"Abby, I ordered your soup and toast. They're rushing it up here, so you've got about fifteen minutes, okay? How are you feeling?"

"Fine." Abby's teeth chattered as she forced her body to stay submerged in the water, with only her head sticking out.

If she could get her fever down, then they could walk through the Christmas market tonight and see the light-and-sound display. She'd bundle up nice and warm and find a place to sit and drink hot chocolate, hopefully by an open fire pit.

That would be the perfect way to end their trip. Not lying in bed for the whole day and night.

She drained the water, thankful to get wrapped up in her robe.

"Feeling better?" Millie asked again while feeling her forehead.

If she had a dollar for every time someone asked her that . . .

Abby crawled into her bed, pulling the covers up over her chest. "While I'm resting this afternoon, you need to go out. All I'm going to do is sleep or watch movies I downloaded. I'll stay in bed from the time you leave till you return. Deal?"

Millie only smiled, that sweet I'm-your-grandmother-so-I'll-do-what-I-want type of smile, and didn't say a word. Not while Millie repacked her suitcase as they waited for room service, not while Abby ate her soup with toast and Millie her salad, and not when Abby snuggled down beneath the comforters and waited for her movie to start.

"All right, your silence is a bit unnerving, Grandmother." Abby eyed Millie with suspicion. "What's going on? I'm in bed, drugged up, and will probably fall sleep before the movie gets interesting. What are you going to do? Watch me all day and read your book?"

Millie checked the time, and when her gaze met Abby's, her eyes sparkled.

"You know, I think you're right. I might just go explore a little. You never know who I'll meet." Millie grabbed her scarf and wrapped it around her neck.

"What? You've got a hot date or something? Wait till David hears about this," Abby teased, and then stretched into a sleepy yawn.

"Oh, I'm sure he won't mind." Millie shrugged on her jacket and reached for her gloves. "Enjoy your nap, love. Have sweet dreams. I may just have a surprise for you when you wake up." She leaned down and gave her a kiss on the forehead. "You don't seem as hot as before—that's good."

"Surprise? Please tell me it has something to do with chocolate." Millie always had the best surprises.

"This is even better. Remember you telling me in Salzburg you had only one wish regarding this trip?"

Abby nodded. She remembered all too well that wish.

That her father would come.

Her breath caught.

Millie nodded.

"Seriously?"

The smile on Millie's face widened.

"They'll be here when you wake. Or they should be." She gave Abby a pointed look. "I can promise you one thing—if they don't catch you sleeping and with that fever gone, there is no way your father will allow you to enjoy the market tonight." She winked before she left the room, leaving Abby to herself.

Abby watched the door close behind her grandmother, heard her sweet laughter as she walked down the hallway, and couldn't stop herself from smiling in response.

If her father was coming, that meant he was okay. Like, really okay. Okay enough to get on a plane and cross the ocean—that type of okay.

And if her father was coming, that meant David was coming too. Which meant Aunt Abigail and Derek were probably following, since there was no way they'd let her father come without them.

Abby closed her computer and set it on the bedside table. She needed to sleep. She needed rest. Whatever her body was fighting, it needed to do that fast and there was no better medicine than sleep.

For once, wouldn't that be nice if it were true? As she had the thought, her body doubled over into a crouch, her face pressed tight into the mattress as a cough tore up through her throat, and her body shook from the sudden chill that ran through her.

Once she caught her breath, she lay back down and let the tears trail down her cheek, drenching the pillow beneath her.

TWENTY-FIVE

CLAIRE

To be read when it's time to tell Abby about Jackson.

Dear Josh,

I know we didn't discuss this, and that's my fault. I kept wanting to bring it up, kept trying, but the words never came.

One day you'll need to tell Abby about Jackson. I don't know what words you'll say to tell her, or even when she'll be ready to know.

I've thought about this letter to you, thought about all the scenarios that could happen, that might happen, that may not happen—and it tears me up inside.

I hate that it's been left to you to tell Abby about Jackson.

I hate that I'm not there to explain what happened and why I made the decisions I did.

I hate that I have no idea whether Jackson is a part of your life, whether that was something he wanted once he turned eighteen or if he decided to maintain his distance.

I hope that Millie continued to stay in touch with him, that she told his adoptive parents about me, about us, about our daughter.

I hope that he is a part of Abby's life, that he is a big brother to her.

Is that wrong of me? To hope that? I know it's not realistic . . . I know that.

I also know that it's not fair that the burden of telling our daughter about the son I gave up so long ago should fall on your shoulders alone, so I have written a letter to Abby to explain it to her . . . but I'm leaving it in your care, along with this letter.

Read it. Then read it with her, read it to her, or let her read it alone—when she is ready.

I have no idea how you will know, but I trust you. You'll know.

I've also shared that I've written this letter with David. I trust David to remain impartial, and I know my mother. If Jackson is still a part of her life, she'll want him to be a part of Abby's, whether they are ready for that or not. David will help balance her. He's good for her even if she doesn't realize that yet. (I really hope they are married by now, that my mother has stopped being so foolish, and that she has realized just how much that man loves her. But if they aren't, I've known David long enough to know he won't let my mother push him to the side. He'll find a way to be part of her life.) You're probably wondering why I didn't leave this with Abigail. I've asked her to do so much already when it comes to our daughter, I didn't want to add this to the list.

I love you, Joshua Turner. I love you with every fiber of my being.

Thank you for doing this. For sharing Jackson with her, for saying the words I can't say, for everything.

I hope that one day you have a relationship with my son. That you'll be able to tell him a day didn't go by without him in my thoughts.

I've thought about writing him a letter . . . just in case. If I do, if you find a letter for him along with this one, could you see that he gets it? Will you tell him that I love him, that I have always loved him and always will?

Thank you.

Forever and always.

xoxo,

Claire

TWENTY-SIX

JOSH

*D*ad, *I need you.*
Four little words that meant the world to him.

Four little words that got him through every single second of the flight, when he wasn't asleep.

Four little words that blasted any panic attack about to start.

His daughter needed him.

It hadn't even been a question—the moment he knew she was sick, he would be there by her side. With Abigail with them, she would know how serious this cold was and whether she needed immediate care or could return home first. He would rather bring her back home, where Dr. JJ could see her rather than some unknown doctor who had no idea about her medical history.

In the cab on their way to the hotel, Abigail stared out the window, clutching Derek's arm at every glimpse she caught of a historic building or tourist sight she wanted to visit. Josh kept checking his phone to see if Abby had left him another message.

Millie said she was sleeping. Hopefully that was the reason for her not responding.

By the time they arrived at the hotel, his anxiety had risen to a level that no doubt affected his blood pressure. He'd already taken a painkiller to dull the throbbing in his head.

Millie waited for them in the lobby, pacing back and forth between the windows and the sitting area. She launched herself at David and welcomed him in a way that made Josh turn his back, grinning with embarrassment along with the others who happened to be in the lobby.

"I'll, um, go get us checked in." Derek shook his head at the two obvious lovebirds.

"Millie?" Josh attempted to interrupt the . . . awkward scene playing out in front of him, but they paid him no attention. *"Millie!"* He raised his voice.

The satisfied smile on Millie's face made Abigail chuckle. Snuggled up tight in David's arms, Millie took a few seconds to return to Earth, to let the dazed look in her eyes subside.

That expression reminded him so much of Claire and how she used to look after he finished kissing her senseless.

"Millie, I hate to break this up, but I need to see my daughter, please?"

"Here." Millie pulled the key card from her pocket. "Room 312. She was still asleep the last time I checked on her."

Josh took the card, hiked his backpack onto his shoulder, and strode to the elevator.

"Josh," Abigail called out to him. "I'll come with you."

He held the elevator open as she made sure Derek had their luggage and knew where she was going.

"Breathe," Abigail said to him after the door closed. "If she's sleeping, that's good."

Josh nodded in silence, his pent-up frustration too powerful for it to feel safe to say anything.

He prayed she was okay. That she'd wake up from this nap feeling better.

They knocked quietly on the door, then used the card to let them-selves in.

Abby lay on the bed, her eyes slowly opening and then staring at them in disbelief.

"Dad?"

Josh rushed over and sat beside her, his hand on her forehead, holding his breath while he waited for the heat of her skin to scorch his hand.

He heaved a big breath of relief at the slightly warm feel. Slightly warm was much better than scorching. Slightly warm meant the fever was going down. Slightly warm was good.

He leaned down and placed a kiss on the top of her head. "Hey, sweetheart." He wound his arm around her shoulders in an awkward hug.

"I can't believe you came." She leaned into his arm, the sweetest smile he could imagine on her face. "But I'm so glad you did."

"I am too." Josh gave her another kiss. He stood to give Abigail room to examine his daughter.

"Hey, Abby." Abigail knelt down and looked Abby in the eyes. "You weren't supposed to get sick, remember? We had a deal."

Josh helped Abby sit up and then stepped back while his friend did what she did best.

Abby looked okay. Her eyes were a bit glassy, her nose red, and her skin was almost as pale as the bedsheets, but he'd seen her worse. Much, much worse.

"How are you feeling, Dad?" Abby asked.

Josh gave her a smile to set her at ease. He knew she was worried about him. She didn't need to be.

"I'm fine, hon. Ask your aunt. No panic attacks once I was on the plane."

Abby looked at her aunt, the question plain on her face. Abigail nodded.

"It's true." She rose and moved to sit on the opposite bed. "And you're not as bad as I'd expected." She reached for the pill bottle she'd given Abby before the trip and shook it. "You've been taking the medicine I gave you, which is good."

Abby pulled her legs beneath her and pushed the comforter off. "I just have a cold, that's all."

Josh scoffed. "So, what, the fever you had earlier was a hallucination?"

Abby blanched. "Millie told you?"

He nodded.

"You have more than a cold, and if we were home, you know where you'd be going right now, right?" Abigail said quietly.

Abby sighed. "I was so hoping, you know? It's been a year . . ." She cleared her throat and coughed, turning her head into the crook of her arm to smother the sound. "I just wanted to make this trip perfect, you know? For Millie. There's still more she wanted to do." She stared down at the floor and her shoulders slumped.

"David's here, so if they want to stay longer, they can. But you and I are headed back first thing tomorrow morning," Josh said.

Abby's head snapped up, a mixture of shock, disappointment, and resignation flashing across her face.

"Dr. JJ is expecting us, Abby." Josh broke the news as softly as he could.

He knew the moment when his words registered.

"Of course she is," she muttered.

"It's for the best." Abigail leaned forward and squeezed Abby's arm.

"So my last day here, in Brussels, is probably going to be spent in this room, isn't it?" Abby asked, her arm reaching behind her neck as she yawned.

Josh went to stand by the window and looked down to the busy street.

"Is being out in the cold, wearing your body out to the point of exhaustion, worth it?" He asked her.

He forced himself to remember that she is an adult, and she had the right to be part of the decision.

Truth be told, she should be the one making the decisions, not him. Except, he couldn't help himself.

When she didn't answer him, he turned and waited, watching her while she looked everywhere but at him.

"Abby?" He prodded.

"Millie and I kind of had a deal," Abby stated. "If I rested today and my fever goes away, then we'd go to the market tonight."

Josh's first response was *hell no,* but he held back and turned toward Abigail instead. He tried to give her a look, *the* look, that said *Say no,* but she ignored him.

"Let's play it by ear. Rest a little more, and we'll talk then, okay?" There was a knock at the door, and Abigail stood to go answer it. "I know it's your last day," she called over her shoulder, "and you want to make it special, but at what cost?"

"How much is what going to cost me?" Derek said as he came in followed by David and Millie. "Our stuff is in our room, which is quite nice by the way, and we've got some time before dinner to relax. And by *relax* I mean . . ." He waggled his eyebrows as he leaned in for a kiss, and laughed when Abigail swatted his arm.

"I'm the one paying the price," Abby said as she climbed out of bed and gave the newcomers a hug. "Welcome to Belgium. The land of chocolate, Smurfs, and—"

"And Belgium waffles." Derek finished for her. "Did you know there's a café right across the road that serves waffles all day? I don't know about you, but I'm kind of starving . . ." He jabbed his wife's side.

"Yeah, I got the hint. Abby, you hungry? Want me to bring you back something to eat? Millie mentioned you had breakfast and then soup, but if you're feeling better, you need more."

"Feed the cold, right?" Abby said.

"You got it. Besides, are you really going to turn down a Belgium waffle?" Abigail blew her a kiss before leaving the room with Derek.

Josh caught Derek's look before leaving. The is-she-really-okay-and-I've-got-your-back look. Josh nodded, giving Derek a thumbs-up.

While David and Abby were in a conversation, Millie came over to join him.

"David told me the plan," Millie said. "How are you doing?" When she laid her hand on his arm and squeezed, Josh covered her hand with his own.

"I'm okay. Better than I thought I would be. David . . . he told me about the letter in Claire's desk."

Millie nodded at that, and Josh figured David had told her already.

"That daughter of yours, she was a one of a kind. Knew me better than I know myself." Josh half turned so he was no longer facing his daughter directly.

"I know what you mean," Millie said in response. "Abby—she's going to be okay."

He couldn't say anything. After all this time, all these years, he knew there was no guarantee.

He used to think that if they could hit that one-year mark without any colds, without any hospital visits, then they'd be in the clear. He could then breathe. Abby could breathe.

But, there was no guarantee. He knew that now.

"I know Abby really wants to experience the market tonight. It's a pretty special one, so I talked with the concierge downstairs, and—"

"She's not spending the night outside in the cold," Josh interrupted her. What was she thinking? Why did she think it would be okay, in any scenario, for Abby to be outside at night, in the middle of winter?

"Josh . . ."

He shook his head. "No."

"Do you trust me?" Millie asked.

Josh didn't know how to answer that. It wasn't really a fair question. Of course he trusted her, but right now, if it was between trusting her and taking care of his daughter, Abby came first. Always.

"Just . . . let's see how Abby does over the rest of the day, okay? Let me work with the concierge here to make this a night Abby will remember. Please?"

Josh watched Abby, the way she rolled her shoulders and rubbed the muscles at the back of her neck, how she didn't stay on her feet for long, but rather sank back down on her bed, looking like she was ready to collapse . . . she needed to be resting and not entertaining.

"No promises, Millie." She was about to debate with him, so he cut her off. "Why don't you and David go for a walk, and I'll stay with Abby. Okay?" He gave her a pointed look, daring her to argue with him.

Her eyes narrowed, but she eventually conceded.

It was nice to be alone with Abby after David and Millie left. He listened to her tell him stories about their trip, about her highlights and the moments she would always remember.

"I remember your mom spending hours writing in that journal. We'd record and watch travel shows on Germany and she'd have that book out and we'd have to pause the television all the time so she could write things down without missing anything."

One of the things he loved was talking about Claire with Abby. He loved sharing his memories, loved telling her stories, keeping her alive in both their hearts.

"Hey, Dad? Can I ask you something?" Abby whispered.

Josh's jaw clenched. "You can ask me anything." He just hoped she didn't ask the wrong question.

"I'm the child of Mom's heart, right?" She watched him, and it took extreme effort to keep his face blank.

"Why do you ask?"

She sighed. He knew it was because he'd answered her question with a question, something she hated.

"I found a postcard in London from Mom, and it was . . . sad. She was really sad. It was a side of her I'd never seen before."

Josh rolled his shoulders and turned his gaze away, not facing her directly.

"Abby, you remember when I said we tried for years before you came along? The last time we went on a trip together, your mom and I . . . we kind of decided to give up trying." He stared up at the ceiling, wishing with all his heart that he didn't have to say anything more.

"So, Mom was saying good-bye basically? To the idea of being a mother?"

Josh nodded.

"It really wasn't me she was writing to then, was it? It was more the child she always dreamed of having, of holding in her arms, of seeing grow up. She was saying good-bye to her dream." Abby's voice broke.

Josh cleared his throat. "You were our miracle." He cleared it again, preparing to tell her the rest.

"That makes sense." Abby's words stopped him. "Sometimes it's easy for me to forget she was also a woman, not just a mom. But, I'm sure there's more . . . there was more to her than just what she wrote in the letters or what I saw in the videos." She sighed. "Why won't anyone tell me?"

He'd made a decision on the plane ride that he wouldn't hold back any more secrets from her. She deserved to know about Jackson. He'd thought about this moment for years, of how to tell her, of whether he even should, since Jackson had never reached out to them . . . But it wasn't fair to Abby. She deserved to know.

"I found a letter from your mom," he said softly.

Abby's eyes lit up. "A new one?"

"It's for you and will answer those questions you have. Would you like to read it or have me read it to you?"

"It's been a long time since you've read me a story, Dad." She gave him a winning smile, reminiscent of when she was a little girl and he'd read to her before bed.

"This might not be the kind of story you're expecting, Abby." He pulled the letter from his pocket and unfolded it, smoothing it across his lap. "Your mom had a secret that not many people knew, and until this letter, she'd never given me any clear way of sharing this secret with you." He looked Abby straight in the eyes, needing her to understand the importance of what he was trying to say.

"So that's why you've never told me? Because Mom didn't tell you to?"

He winced. "Well, no, not exactly," he said. "There never seemed like a good time to tell you—we've always been focused on other things . . ." He glanced down at the letter. "But that's not an excuse."

"But you're telling me now."

He nodded. "I'm sorry that I waited so long. I know you'll have lots of questions, and I won't have all the answers. But"—he swallowed what felt like a handful of nails—"let's just read this first, okay?"

> *Dear Abby,*
>
> *I want to tell you a story. My story. From a time before I met your father, from a time when I was a girl with a heavy heart. It's not a sad story, but it's not a happy one either. It's just . . . a story. Of life, of loss, and of love.*
>
> *One night I made a decision. It wasn't a good decision or a bad decision, it was just a decision made in the heat of the moment, a decision that changed my life.*
>
> *I was a teenager who didn't understand what life was all about. A teenager who ended up pregnant and who had a father who didn't think keeping the baby was a smart decision.*
>
> *I didn't have the best of relationships with my father, Abby. We rarely saw eye to eye, and after I became*

pregnant, I would even go so far as to say that any love I
had for him disappeared when he demanded that I have
an abortion.

I didn't. I refused. Instead I went and hid myself in
the family cottage for the duration of my pregnancy, hid
myself so my father wouldn't have to admit to those he
knew that I wasn't perfect, so that no one would know
about my baby, and he would save face. See, my father
was an important man in our town, and his reputation
meant more to him than my happiness.

He was not a man I would want you to call
grandfather.

During those months at the family cabin, I grew to
love the child I carried. I tried to dream about a future
for the two of us, of what life could be like if I defied
my parents and kept my baby. Unfortunately, I was only
a teenager with no plans for the future, no career that
would support us, and no family who would help us
along. My mother came and stayed with me, helped me
through those months, took care of me, and loved me as
only a mother can. And she helped me to realize that the
life I would be giving my child wouldn't be the best life
for him, and that's what my child deserved—the best life
possible.

It was hard to give my child up for adoption. It was
hard to agree to let others love him and raise him as their
own. It was hard to step away and know I might never
see him again. It was the worst time of my life, and there
is a part of me that has never healed.

For one hour, I was a mother. For one hour, I held
and loved my son. My son was named Jackson, and from
that moment on, all I ever wanted was for him to be

happy and loved. And the most loving action I could take as his mother was to find others who could give him a better life than I could.

That hour, my sweet Abby, helped me to realize what being a mother is all about. It's about placing your child's life first, doing everything and anything I can to ensure my baby grows up knowing what love is, and being safe and protected.

That hour, it helped me to make the decision I did for you—to put you first, to make sure you have enough time to grow before I go for treatment for my cancer. Regardless of whether it worked for me or not, I know it is the right decision to make. You are my everything. For you, I will do anything and everything to ensure you are born healthy and strong.

I hope that one day you will meet Jackson. I know my mother has kept in touch with him and his adoptive family, so if one day you decide you want to build a relationship with him, I believe she can help you. I don't know if it will happen, but I hope it does. If that's what you want. If that's what he wants.

I love you, Abigail Marie Turner. I love you with all my heart, and I pray that when you read this letter, you won't hate me or question my love for you in any way.

Forever and always,
Your mom

By the time he finished reading, his voice was hoarse from unshed tears. When he looked over at Abby, her eyes were closed, but he could see the dampness on her pillow.

"He's the child of her heart, isn't he? I always thought it was me, but . . ." Her voice trailed off, and Josh didn't have the words to ease that pain she must be feeling.

So he said nothing, just sat by her side, stroking her hair as the tears continued to flow down her cheek and onto her pillow.

"Do you know him? Jackson? Do you talk to him? See him?" Abby finally asked.

Josh shook his head.

"I've never met or spoken to him," he admitted. He caught the look of relief on Abby's face and realized she must have assumed he'd kept that from her too. "I've seen his photo, though. Millie shared it with your mom before you were born." No more secrets. Not if he could help it.

"Her father sounds horrible. I'm glad"—she yawned and blindly reached out for his hand, holding on tight—"I'm glad that we don't have that type of relationship," she said quietly.

He leaned over and kissed her forehead. "So am I," he whispered.

"Does he know about me?" The words slurred together.

From the way her lashes fluttered, he could tell she was fighting to stay awake. He knew there was so much more to say, to explain, but she needed her sleep more than she needed those answers.

Did Jackson know about her? Yes, he knew. Millie had let him know the news of both Claire's death and the birth of Abby. She'd sent a few photos throughout the years, but that's as far as it ever went.

"Go to sleep love, okay? I'll be right here by your side when you wake up. We can talk about this later," he said quietly.

A soft smile graced her face, and he wiped her tears away with a tissue. He didn't leave her side until he knew she was fast asleep and only then to sit in the chair in the corner, where he could look down to the street below.

He needed to get her home, so she could get the care she needed to fight off this cold. They had a rough few weeks ahead of them while she recovered, but that pain in his heart of not knowing how she was, whether she was going to be okay or not, was ebbing. He was here with her, by her side in a country he'd once visited with Claire. And he was okay.

Maybe if he'd had the courage to face his fear none of this would have happened. He could have brought her himself during the summer months, when the weather wasn't problematic and her lungs could function properly.

He couldn't focus on that right now, though. He was here, he'd survived without crumbling into a panic attack, and he had a plan in place to take Abby home to get her the care she needed.

All that mattered was his daughter. If he'd learned anything from Claire, it was that.

He would do anything and everything for Abby. No matter the cost.

TWENTY-SEVEN

ABBY

Abby's Journey: A Personal Blog

Trip of a Lifetime: Last Day

Quick status update. My family is here. On my last day in Europe, my whole family decided to surprise me and showed up in my hotel room.

Dad and I leave first thing tomorrow morning, and then it's a trip to the hospital for me. Again. But Millie and David, and Aunt Abigail and Derek will be staying behind, enjoying their time here in beautiful Brussels (or wherever their heart's desire takes them—a quick hop on the train, and they could be in a new country within hours . . . like, for realz, people. Can you imagine!)

*I've loved every moment of this trip. It's been
a dream come true in more ways than one.
The best part has been seeing a small section
of Europe through the eyes of my mother.*

I'll be back. You can be sure.

*PS. Millie just told me to say I'll be scratching
a few more things off my list tonight—but
it's a surprise, so I'll tell you about it in a few
days!*

"Are you ready?" Millie stamped her feet in either anticipation or frustration, Abby wasn't sure.

"I've been ready for the past hour, Millie," Abby grumbled. She gave her aunt a very pointed look, added in a frown, and ignored the smile she received back.

"Fever is gone. You've eaten. You're bundled up tight. I think we're ready. Josh?"

Abby, along with everyone else in the room, looked at her father.

He just rolled his eyes and wrapped his baby-blue scarf, the one Abby knitted for him last Christmas, around his neck.

"Fine. But I'm watching you, Abigail Turner, and the minute I see a goose bump, a shiver, or a red nose, we're coming straight back to this hotel. Got it?" He held up two fingers and motioned from his eyes to her—the I'm-watching-you gesture.

"It's winter, and there's a chill in the air, of course her nose is going to get red," Derek grumbled before he took Abby's hand and pulled her out of the room. "If you don't come now, we'll never get out of there." With a conspiratorial twinkle in his eye, he drew her down the hallway, so they were the first to arrive at the elevators.

"Any idea what Millie has planned?" She asked him while they waited.

"Oh, I know everything that's been planned." His smile grew from cheek to cheek. "You're going to love it."

Every cell in Abby's body thrummed with excitement. It had from the moment Millie told her to get ready for a night out on the square. She pushed aside everything she'd learned in that letter. She didn't want to focus on it, to think about the words or what they meant, or let it ruin her last night here.

"Miss Abby?" A member of the concierge team waited for them in the lobby. Abby glanced over at Millie, who nodded, eyes wide with excitement.

"Yes?"

"I'm Stefan, your concierge, and it's been a pleasure to work with your grandmother today to make this night as perfect as we could." He held out his hand for Abby to take.

"Perfect, eh?"

"Oh, you Canadians . . ." Stefan laughed as he led them to the front doors. Abby peeked around him to find a horse-drawn carriage—no, make that two carriages.

"Your evening begins here. These carriages are heated, so you won't get too cold. Our drivers will take you around the city, showing you our enchanting city at night before coming back to the market. There, we've booked a private seating area for you to spend the rest of the evening. You'll be able to see our beautiful Christmas tree as well as watch the display on the Grand Place while keeping warm." He pushed the door open for them. "I hear you are heading home tomorrow, so we wanted to make your last night with us as memorable and magical as possible for you." He leaned toward Millie and said, "The seating area is booked for three hours."

They took a few minutes to say hi to their drivers, to pet the horses, and then split up into two groups. Millie and David took one carriage for themselves, while the rest climbed into the other. The inside was quite nice with plush seats and throw blankets for everyone.

Derek let out a low whistle. "I don't even want to think about how much this cost." He draped a blanket over his wife's legs and held his own in his lap.

"Tonight is a gift from Millie and David." Josh tucked Abby's blanket snug around her legs and she let him without complaint. She knew she should probably be in bed, but she was so glad both her aunt and her father gave in and let her have this last night.

She was already exhausted, and they'd only just started their carriage ride. She had no doubt that if she begged to call it an early night, her father would be all over that. As long as she could sit and listen to the music, capture the light show on video, watch her grandparents snuggle up together, and picture her mother here enjoying all of this . . . she would be happy.

She stared out the window, trying hard to smother her cough, knowing everyone in the carriage heard her.

She didn't dare look at anyone, didn't want to see the concern in their eyes, didn't want to hear them ask if she was okay.

She didn't want to admit that her chest hurt more than she'd admitted earlier. That she knew she should be in bed.

It was hard, knowing that by this time tomorrow night, she'd be back in the hospital, getting prodded and poked and having Dr. JJ give her the "You need to take better care of your body, and we've talked about this before" speech.

It was hard, knowing that everyone right now was more than willing to put her health first, that they were all trying very hard to temper their excitement about being here in Brussels.

It was hard, knowing that her father took a step in the right direction, and that it was only temporary. She wished it could be for longer, that they could stay here and travel, that he could show her the places he'd visited with her mom years ago.

It was hard, living in the moment when the moment was fleeting.

But she would do it. Because that's what her mother had done, all those years ago.

She would make her mom proud. Because this moment mattered.

TWENTY-EIGHT

ABBY

Two Weeks Later

Abby's Journey: A Personal Blog

Home from the Hospital

There's no place like home. There's no place like home. There's no place like home. I'm clicking the heels of my red slippers and so thankful to be back in my own bed, eating real food and surrounded by those I love most (that's not to say I don't like the nurses at the hospital, but I could do without seeing them again for a while . . .).

I came home to the best welcome present a girl could ask for. Homemade soup, my favorite casseroles, and cake. Lots of cake. The best way to beat a cold is to feed it, right? I think we can safely say, thanks to awesome cooks here in Heritage, we'll kill this cold with homemade love.

My grandparents will be home today—they stayed behind in Brussels, and I can't wait to see them. Mainly I want the gifts they're sure to have bought for me . . . yes, I realize I'm no longer a child, but who doesn't love presents?

Abby rested on the couch in their living room, her feet on top of her father's knees as they rewatched the Smurf cartoons he'd given her as a Christmas gift last year. The bowl of popcorn held only a few kernels, and her mug of tea had grown cold. She'd written half a dozen thank-you notes already for the delicious soups and baked goods that people had left for them when they came home, and she was exhausted.

She'd been home for the whole day, promising Dr. JJ she would relax and do nothing to exert any more energy than was absolutely necessary. She was tired and would drop off to sleep at any time, but she couldn't. She tapped her fingers against the side of the couch.

Millie and David were coming home today.

"You're fidgety," Sam said from across the room.

Abby chuckled. "You can barely see me from over there, so how would you know?" The look Sam gave her made Abby wheeze as she tried to suppress her laughter, which in turn produced a frown of her father's face. He pointed to the inhaler in Abby's lap, which she quickly used.

"Behave yourselves," her father warned, his tone more stern than she'd heard in the last few days.

Her dad had sat by her side the whole week while she lay in that hospital bed. She'd expected to hear him say things like *I told you so* or *Next time maybe listen to me*, but he said nothing like that.

Instead, he asked her questions about her trip and listened to her stories of the markets. She shared with him what she'd read in her mom's journal. And then, they talked about Jackson.

Abby had so many questions, and it had been hard to hear the lack of answers from her father. He asked her to be patient, to wait till Millie came home, but that had been harder than she'd thought.

She'd read and reread her mother's letter so many times. She'd been upset and frustrated that the existence of her half brother had been kept from her for so long.

"What's going through that head of yours?" Sam asked.

Abby glanced at her father but he stared at the television.

"I wish Millie and David would hurry up, you know? They must be home by now." Abby checked her phone. She'd texted her grandmother hours ago but hadn't heard anything back yet.

Millie promised to bring over a letter Jackson had sent her years ago. A letter for her to read when she was ready to know more about him.

The moment she'd found out about the letter, she'd rolled her eyes. *Of course* he'd write a letter. Except, it would have been nice if she'd been given an e-mail address or phone number. She wanted to know her half brother, wanted to talk to him, find out about his life. She'd tried to look him up online, but all she knew was his first name and that led nowhere.

Their mother called him Jackson.

His adoptive mother calls him Jack.

She had so many questions about him. He would be thirty-six years old, probably had a family of his own, with daughters or sons keeping him busy. Was he an artist like her mother or did he go into a completely different field? Where did he live? Was it close by or across the country or maybe across the world? Did he have the same desire to travel or was he a homebody? How tall was he? Did he look like their mom or did he take after his birth father more?

How weird was it to think of her mom as *their* mom?

"You're anxious for the letter, aren't you?" Sam wasn't really into small talk today. Ever since she'd arrived last night she'd went for the hard questions, not letting Abby get away with pat answers about how she was feeling.

"Well, I think I'll go check to make sure there's beer in the fridge for when David arrives," her dad said. He cleared his throat and eased her feet off his legs. "Anyone want anything? More popcorn? More tea? Another piece of cake?"

Abby raised her hand. "If there's another coconut cupcake, I'll take that."

"I'm good. Dean should be here in a few minutes."

"Why don't I pack up some treats for you for the road—and how about one of the casseroles?" He didn't bother to wait for Sam's reply, just walked into the kitchen, whistling the Smurf theme song.

Sam came and sat beside her on the couch and reached for her hand. "No matter what's in that letter, it'll all be okay."

Abby winced. "I hope so." Her stomach churned at the idea. She rolled her shoulders to relieve some of the tension and muted the sound on the television.

"What if the letter is a brush-off? What if he doesn't want to get to know me?" She voiced her strongest concern and waited for Sam to tell her she was being overly apprehensive.

Except Sam didn't say anything. She pulled her legs up beneath herself and shrugged.

"This is where you tell me that of course he'll want to get to know me," Abby mentioned.

Sam squeezed her hand. "I would love to tell you that, honey, but what if he doesn't? Maybe he's happy with his life and just wishes you well? Are you ready for that? I don't want to be the killjoy here, but—"

"Too late for that," Abby grumbled. What was Sam's problem?

"But, I'd hate for you to build up expectations about this idealized man only to be devastated if he destroys your dreams of him being a part of your life." Sam ignored her tone.

Abby thought about that. Thought about the possibility that maybe he really didn't care to know her. She'd often thought about why he'd never reached out. If she found out she'd been adopted, the first thing she would do would be to search out her birth mother, right?

"I think that depends," Sam said softly.

Abby flushed. She hadn't meant to say it out loud.

"You wouldn't want to know your history? Who your birth mother was? Find out why she gave you up for adoption?" Abby asked. She would. That would be the first thing she did the moment she found out.

Sam shook her head. "Not if I have a good relationship with my parents. Sure, I'd be curious, and I'd ask a lot of questions, but I'd weigh the costs too. Would it be a betrayal to the parents who raised me? If there were health concerns, then yes, I'd want to know my history. But I'm not sure I'd have that deep need to know why someone gave me up. You know?"

Abby sighed. "You're right," she said. "I guess it depends on the person. I mean, I think I would *need* to know, and I'd hope that my dad would support me in that."

"But what if he didn't? Or what if he said he did, but you knew how much it hurt him to find out he wasn't enough for you?" Sam asked.

"Of course he is." Abby hadn't thought of it like that. That bothered her. She wouldn't want to hurt her dad like that.

"I'm just saying," Sam said gently, "there could be any number of reasons why he hasn't reached out until now. You should be prepared."

Abby leaned back and closed her eyes. She heard what Sam was saying. She did. And she understood the truth of it as well, but there was a part of her—okay, a large part of her—that hoped Sam was being excessively wary.

Specks, Sam's dog, rose from her spot on the floor and went to stand by the door, giving one short bark.

The grin on Sam's face at Specks's bark took Abby's breath away—which wasn't hard since she was still short of breath. Dean must be here. He'd trained the dog to bark like that so Sam would know when he arrived to pick her up.

"You need to marry that man sooner rather than later," Abby said.

"What about our plan to get an apartment?" Sam crouched in front of the couch and placed both hands on Abby's face. "I love Dean, but I know how much you need some independence." She said it quietly as Abby's dad walked from the kitchen toward the front door.

It was time for Abby to face reality. She wasn't going anywhere for the next little while.

"Don't put your life on hold for me," she said. "Let's face it, the likelihood of my father letting me out of his sight for the next five years is close to nil," she said playfully, knowing her dad was listening.

"I heard that," he called out. She heard the door open, and a bevy of voices greeted him. It sounded like Millie and David were here as well.

For the next few minutes, things were boisterous with Sam getting ready to leave, Dean coming over to check on her on the way to grabbing Sam's bags, and Millie and David raising a ruckus over her not being in bed or sipping a hot cup of tea.

It was heaven on earth, and Abby loved every moment of the chaos.

It took almost a half hour before Millie and David had settled down and Sam left for home with Dean. David had brought a new tea blend with a peppermint taste, which Abby enjoyed.

"Be honest with me, Abby. Are you feeling okay? Should you have come home sooner? Was it worth it?" Millie sat at the edge of her chair, a warm mug of coffee between her hands, and gave Abby her full attention.

"I'm feeling okay, Millie, truly. I'm exhausted, but I'll be fine. And yes, it was worth every moment," Abby confirmed. She wouldn't have changed anything about the trip—well, maybe the part about getting sick—but she planned on carrying those memories with her for a very long time. "I can't wait to go back."

She glanced at her father as she said that. She'd been trying to talk him into going with her to the south of France, or even Italy to visit Rocco and Miima, but so far, he refused to agree to any of it, saying they'd have to see how she was feeling.

She hated that response.

Millie reached down and took an envelope from her purse. "I have a feeling you've been waiting for this, haven't you? Jackson wrote this when you were eighteen, so it's a couple years old."

Abby swallowed past the lump in her throat and only nodded.

"I imagine you have a lot of questions, and I promise to answer as many as I can when you are ready." She leaned forward and handed the letter to Abby's dad, who then placed it in her hands.

As she held the envelope, her hands shook slightly and there was a feeling of panic beginning to rise in her. Should she read it now, read it out loud, wait until she was alone? Did she want to read it now? What if . . . what if she didn't like what her half brother said?

She really didn't want to read it with everyone watching.

As if noticing her hesitation, her dad pushed himself up from the couch and motioned to Millie and David to join him. "You should stay for dinner. Millie, we've got an overflowing fridge and freezer that you're more than welcome to look through and raid for some dishes to take home. And David, I know there's a coffee cake with your name on it."

The moment he winked at her, Abby knew he was giving her the space she needed to read the letter. She took in a few deep breaths, the last one causing her to cough, which prompted her dad to rush in from the kitchen faster than she'd expected.

"I'm okay," she managed to whisper.

"Are you sure?"

She nodded and waved him away, pausing until her pounding heart slowed before opening the envelope.

She didn't read the words at first, just stared at the way they were written. Straight lines, printed letters, stoic and strong—that was the feeling she got when looking at the penmanship. It was unlike her mothers, which was always cursive and soft.

She looked for his signature and smiled to herself. *Jack.* He called himself Jack, just like the books her parents wrote together. She speculated about what her mom would have thought of that and wondered if anyone saw the parallels there—her mother drawing illustration upon illustration of a boy she imagined in her head, but who was real in her heart. She would need to talk to her father about that, ask him if he'd known about her son when they first created the series together. She had a feeling he did.

> *Abby,*
>
> *Letters like these are never easy, and to be honest, I'm not much of a letter person, something my wife can attest to, since I've written her a total of two since we first met over twelve years ago.*
>
> *Today is your eighteenth birthday. I'm not sure when you'll read this, but hopefully, it will be sooner rather than later.*
>
> *I've thought a lot about what to say, how to introduce myself or attempt to explain why it's taken me so long to contact you, and I've realized there will never be the right words to say it, so I might as well bumble my way through as best I can.*

My name is Jack Cole. I'm an architect with a degree in design. My wife, Hailey, is a video game programmer for games for children, and we have our own test subjects named Elijah and Reagan, who are seven-year-old twins. I live on coffee and have been known to make a pretty decent coconut cream pie. I have an older sister, Taylor, and my parents are Steven and Marie. They didn't tell me I was adopted until I was eighteen—that's when I received my first letter from Millie and found out about Claire and about you.

My mother and Millie have kept in contact throughout the years. It was Millie who first told me about your blog, and I catch up on what you've been doing every Sunday morning. It's actually a tradition now for the whole family. We snuggle up on the bed, the kids by my side, and we read out loud the words you share with us about your life (I hope that doesn't creep you out). I can't imagine what it would be like to basically grow up in a hospital. I also can't imagine what your father must feel—I always think about how I would handle it as a father, and truth be told, I'd be a basket case (Hailey is nodding her head—she's the strong one between us). Reagan has a book full of pictures she's drawn for you, and Elijah wonders if you like to play video games—he thinks that would be a great way to spend the time when you're sick.

You probably want to know why I haven't contacted you until now. That's a hard question to answer, but I'll try to explain it. I thought about how I felt, finding out that I was adopted, at eighteen. It changed my life, left me with so many questions with very few answers. I didn't

think it would be fair for you to deal with my existence
on top of everything else you were dealing with. I didn't
want to add on extra stress, especially when it seemed like
you already had a lot to handle. I also didn't want to force
my way into your life, which is why I asked Millie to not
share this letter until you found out about me and wanted
to know more—even if that day never comes.

I'm here, a brother that would like to know his sister,
Jack

By the time Abby was done reading the letter, heavy tears streamed down her face, and she reread it over and over and then hugged it close to her heart. She had a brother who wanted to know her. He really wanted to know her.

Questions? She had so many. But right now, she just wanted to savor this moment.

Life wasn't always easy and there were a lot of bumps in the journey she'd taken so far, but there were a lot of highlights too. This was one of them.

TWENTY-NINE

CLAIRE

Dear Josh and Abby,
All I ever wanted was a family.

Family means unconditional love and acceptance, where you are valued as a person and your opinions and beliefs matter.

Family means celebrating the good days and being there for the days that aren't so good.

Family isn't just those related to you by blood. It's those you love and who love you back.

Looking back, I realize that family also means admitting no one is perfect, accepting the mistakes and decisions made by others, no matter how hard that is. With that in mind . . . . I'm hoping by now you'll have forgiven me.

It's hard to write this letter because I know that it must seem like I've given up on my family, but believe me when I tell you that all I ever wanted was the best for you both.

I want to be the best mother I can be to you, Abby. Which means placing your life above my own.

I want to be the best wife I can be for you, Josh. Which means giving you the opportunity to have one of your own dreams come true—to be a father.

As I write this, I hope, pray, and even believe that everything will turn out fine, that we can grow up to be a family together. But there's one thing I've learned—life doesn't always happen the way we hope it will.

So, in case I can't say this in person:

Always say I love you *to each other, even if things get tough between you.*

Forgive before you condemn.

Be willing to listen, no matter how hard it hurts to hear the truth.

Always tell the truth. Lies are never worth the cost.

Don't be afraid to consider a future not of your own making. Change is okay.

No one and no thing—even your reputation—is worth more than you are to each other.

Be the best family you can be for each other. I love you. I love you both more than you could possibly imagine, and it has been my greatest honor to be called your wife and to be your mother.

Always and forever,

Claire

ACKNOWLEDGMENTS

It often takes a community to write a story worth telling, and I'm so thankful for those who have helped me with this journey.

A very special thank you to Marlene Roberts Engel. It has been a privilege to write my Sam and name her after your precious daughter, who passed away too young.

I'm thankful to know one of the best pediatric intensive care physicians in Calgary—Dr. Jaime Blackwood. Thank you for answering my countless questions. And I'm so proud to say I knew you back when we were just kids in a small-town school. Any and all errors related to any medical treatment or terminology are solely mine.

I have the best readers, and I can't thank you enough for all your support, your help when I ask questions, and for believing in me and loving my stories like you do!

I love having children old enough to make dinner and a husband who doesn't mind all my traveling. Once again, I could not have written this book without you. One of the best memories I have of writing this book was my research trip to Germany to experience the Christmas markets firsthand with my middle daughter. It was a trip of a lifetime, something for the memory books! Thanks for being a great travel partner, Ayla!

ABOUT THE AUTHOR

Steena Holmes is the *New York Times* and *USA Today* bestselling author of the novels *Saving Abby*, *The Word Game*, *Stillwater Rising*, *The Memory Child*, *Emma's Secret*, and *Finding Emma*, among others. She won the National Indie Excellence Award in 2012 for *Finding Emma* as well as the USA Book News Award for *The Word Game*. Steena lives in Calgary, Alberta, and continues to write stories that touch every parent's heart. To find out more about her books and her love of traveling, you can visit her website at www.steenaholmes.com or follow her journeys at www.steenatravels.com and on Instagram @steenaholmes.

Photo © 2013 Vanessa Pressacco